D0582127

Lexi was about to wrangle a shark in his surf.

But she had no choice. He might well be Jazi's father—the only person with the power to grant her custody.

A confirmed bachelor, he'd stated in one article she'd read that he never intended to have a family. According to him, he took a satisfaction from his work that he'd never found in a relationship, so why force something that wasn't meant to be?

Lexi hoped he believed what he'd said. Jazi's future rested in his hands. But she needed to confirm her hunch before she put her proposition to him.

She made her way to the bar, a room dressed in dark leather, light wood and shining crystal. And there he was. Seated at the end of the bar in a custom-made tuxedo that emphasized the broad reach of his shoulders, showcasing his tall, lean frame to perfection. His brooding expression kept everyone, including the bartender, at bay.

A shark surveying his territory.

There was nothing subdued about him. His hair was nearly black, his eyes dark and piercing, though the color was indiscernible at this distance and angle. Features a shade too sharp to be considered classically handsome made him all the more compelling.

Dear Reader,

I'm lucky to have a large, very supportive family. If you read my books with any frequency I'm sure that's shown through in my stories, as family always plays a large part in my work. I am aware, however, that not all people are as lucky as me. Sometimes we have to make tough decisions to remove ourselves from harsh or unhealthy situations. Or step back so someone else can flourish.

These decisions don't come easily. They require thought, courage, selfishness, sacrifice, and the bravery necessary to take action. In *The CEO's Surprise Family* an executive faces tough decisions against the backdrop of glittering Las Vegas in a hotel designed after a game. In this world of flash and chance he must choose between giving up the daughter he never knew he had so she can have the kind of life he never did, and going against the odds by accepting love into his life and scoring the biggest jackpot of all: a family of his own.

I hope you hear the *cha-ching* at the end!

Enjoy.

Teresa Carpenter

THE CEO'S SURPRISE FAMILY

BY
TERESA CARPENTER

Published in Great Britain 2016
By Mills & Boon, an imprint of HarperCollins*Publishers*
1 London Bridge Street, London, SE1 9GF

© 2016 Teresa Carpenter

ISBN: 978-0-263-06529-9

Our policy is to use papers that are natural, renewable and recyclable
products and made from wood grown in sustainable forests. The logging
and manufacturing processes conform to the legal environmental
regulations of the country of origin.

Printed and bound in Great Britain
by CPI Antony Rowe, Chippenham, Wiltshire

Teresa Carpenter believes that with love and family anything is possible. She writes in a Southern California coastal city surrounded by her large family. Teresa loves writing about babies and grandmas. Her books have rated as Top Picks by *RT Book Reviews* and have been nominated Best Romance of the Year on some review sites. If she's not at a family event, she's reading or writing her next grand romance.

Books by Teresa Carpenter

Mills & Boon Romance

The Sheriff's Doorstep Baby
The Making of a Princess
Stolen Kiss From a Prince
Her Boss by Arrangement
A Pregnancy, a Party & a Proposal
His Unforgettable Fiancée

Visit the Author Profile page
at millsandboon.co.uk for more titles.

To my readers. Thank you for taking the time
to find me and read me.
And a warm hug to those who go to Amazon
and Goodreads to leave reviews.
You help other readers to find me. Bless you.

CHAPTER ONE

LEXI MALONE'S HAND shook as she touched up her lip liner. She met her gaze in the gilded ladies' room mirror and saw nerves reflected in the blue depths.

"For Jazi," she breathed and capped the liner.

The reminder chased the shakes away. And most of the nerves. She'd do anything to get her twenty-three-month-old goddaughter back. Accosting a man in an upscale restaurant to determine if he was the child's father was nothing. And it may not come to that. Tonight was a fact-finding mission.

At the theater where she'd used to dance strange men had approached her all the time. She'd learned to handle them long ago. Of course, the Golden Link was a well-respected private club at the Golden Cuff Casino and security had stood ready to protect her if things got out of control.

Here all the security belonged to Jethro Calder, a top executive of the Pinnacle Group, and owner of the restaurant she stood in. The Beacon mixed old-world elegance with modern efficiency and hearty fare. And it was housed in the Pinnacle Casino and Hotel where Calder had a penthouse suite.

She was about to wrangle a shark in his surf.

But she had no choice. He may well be Jazi's father, and the only person with the power to grant her custody.

She'd done her homework once she realized his possible relationship to Jazi.

One of the "Fabulous Four" to take Pinnacle Enterprises to the top of the fiercely competitive world of digital gaming, Calder was known as the Dark Predator. Few went up against him without feeling his bite.

A confirmed bachelor, he'd stated in one article that he never intended to have a family. According to him, he took a satisfaction in his work that he'd never found in a relationship so why force something that wasn't meant to be.

Lexi hoped he believed what he said. Jazi's and her futures rested in his hands. But she needed to confirm her hunch before she put her proposition to him. She needed to see his birthmark for herself.

"So stop stalling." She scolded her reflection, earning an odd look from the woman next to her at the vanity. She offered a small smile but the woman tucked her lipstick away and left the bathroom. "Good job, Lexi, you're scaring the tourists."

She sighed, fluffed up her shoulder-length red hair, lifted her chin and followed the woman out. "For Jazi."

It seemed prophetic that today was Alliyah's birthday. Lexi hoped it meant she'd be lucky. She made her way to the bar, a room dressed in dark leather, light wood and shining crystal. Alliyah, Lexi's best friend and Jazi's mother, had been a dancer too. Unlike Lexi, Alliyah had made extra money by being an executive escort. When men like Calder needed a date for an event, they called the service and Alliyah got an expensive night out on the town and earned the money to buy whatever she had her eye on, which could be anything from diapers to a new designer purse.

Sex was not part of the service. But occasionally Alliyah hooked up with her dates. Jazi was the result of one of those hookups. As soon as she'd found out she was pregnant Alliyah had quit the service. Unfortunately, she hadn't been sure of whom the father was. Or more probably she hadn't wanted to share Jazi. Whichever, she'd been closedmouthed about the baby's father, even to Lexi. When she'd died in an automobile accident, her silence contributed to placing her daughter in foster care. A system Alliyah had despised, having bounced around in it for a good part of her youth.

Lexi supposed she could thank her mother for being spared that unpleasant experience. No, Lexi had longed for a little neglect in her childhood. Instead, every moment of every day had been structured, filled with practice, schooling, practice, regimented exercise, practice, scheduled meals, and more practice. All under the strict eye of her mother.

Oh, yeah, Lexi had prayed for time alone.

But that had been a lifetime ago. Now she just wanted custody of her goddaughter, and Jethro Calder was her ticket.

And there he was. Seated at the end of the bar in a custom-made tuxedo that emphasized the broad reach of his shoulders, showcasing his tall, lean frame to perfection. His brooding expression kept everyone, including the bartender at bay.

A shark surveying his territory, there was nothing subdued about him. His hair was nearly black, his eyes dark and piercing, the color indiscernible at this distance and angle. Features a shade too sharp to be considered classically handsome made him all the more compelling.

Pretending uninterest, she studied him in the mirror as she walked up to the bar. "A dirty Manhattan, please," she ordered from the attentive bartender. She held her breath—no going back now. The drink order was a signal to Jethro Calder that she was his date from Excursions.

After reading the article, she'd contacted Sally Easton, the owner of Excursions. Lexi had met the older woman several times when Alliyah worked for her. Sally had even tried to recruit Lexi more than once. Lexi had explained she needed to talk to Calder about something important but when she tried going through his company she got passed on to a lower executive. Sally put Lexi off not wanting to jeopardize his business with Excursions. But today she'd got a call that Jethro Calder's date had to cancel. Sally was giving her this one chance.

"May I buy that for you?" A man old enough to be her father slid onto the stool next to her and leaned into her space.

She controlled the urge to flinch away from him. Why did a miniskirt make men lose all sense of propriety? Before she could politely refuse his none-too-subtle come-on, a tuxedoed arm threaded between them and a deep male voice declared, "She's with me."

A strong hand settled over Lexi's and Jethro Calder assisted her from her seat.

"You're late," he said.

She froze. Then forced herself to relax. She meant to observe him tonight, try to catch a glimpse of the birthmark on his wrist to confirm his link to Jazi and get to know him a little better before retreating to plan her next course of action.

"Right on time actually."

Her gaze went to the mirror making sure no one spotted her for the fraud she was. No one appeared to be paying particular interest in them except a familiar brunette who was lovely but about ten years older than Calder, who she knew to be thirty-five. A cougar on the prowl?

"No way, Calder." Her would-be suitor protested. "You're always claiming the young, pretty ones. If she were with you, why didn't she join you?"

Calder ignored the man. Instead he addressed the bartender, who arrived with her drink. "Sam, Madison's tab is on the house tonight."

"We're having a bit of a tiff." Lexi curled her arm around Calder's. Hard muscles flexed under her fingers.

Slightly mollified by Calder's generosity, Madison's scowl deepened at her gesture. Not wanting his annoyance to turn to suspicion, Lexi grabbed the drink from the bar.

"There are lots of beautiful women here tonight." She set the glass down in front of the brunette whose hair Lexi had styled less than an hour ago. With a smile she announced, "This gentleman would like to buy you a drink."

The woman frowned. The man sputtered. And Calder led Lexi away.

"You're late," he repeated, his breath whispering over her ear, his deep voice shivering over her senses. A warm hand in the small of her back directed her to the elevator that would take them down one floor to the casino floor. "I'll let it slide because watching you hand Madison's ex-wife that drink was the most fun I've had all day."

She eyed his solemn expression. This was him having fun?

"That was his ex-wife?" No wonder she seemed so interested in their interaction.

"Yes. She eats at the restaurant every Friday night after her spa treatment."

"And he comes in every Friday night to pick up pretty young things in front of her?"

"Every week for the last six months."

"People are strange."

"You have no idea how strange until you've lived in a casino."

"Believe me, working in a casino is as close as you need to get to see strange." She'd learned that as a dancer. But that was in the past. Now she cut and styled hair, a day job so she could be at home with Jazi when she got custody.

His eyes narrowed on her. "You work in a casino?" They were a dark, twilight blue. Her heart pounded. She'd only ever seen one other person with eyes that color. Jazi had his eyes. She swallowed in a suddenly dry throat. She'd found Jazi's father.

A hundred emotions rushed through her, love for her goddaughter, hope, fear, anticipation, trepidation. But she forced herself to concentrate on the conversation. "Hasn't everyone who lives in Las Vegas worked at a casino at some point?"

"That doesn't answer my question," he stated.

"I work at Pinnacle's actually. At the Modern Goddess Salon." She wasn't surprised he didn't know her. The spa rented the space. "Is that going to be a problem?"

His brows contracted and she realized he was actually thinking about it. He sighed. "No. It's not a problem."

"I was a last-minute replacement." Lexi advised him, sticking as close to the truth as possible. "I'm afraid I don't know anything about where we're going."

"I never reveal the destination until we're en route."

Of course not. Everything she'd read on the man indicated he was a very private man. He walked with purpose and speed. Luckily her dancer's grace allowed her to keep pace.

"Hmm. Kind of makes it hard to know how to dress."

The fact he wore a tuxedo meant the occasion was formal. She tugged at the hem of her black minidress, hoping she met his requirements.

"I provided the information that it was a formal event." His dark gaze ran over her, the intensity in the navy depths sent a shiver down her spine. "You'll do."

"Good to know."

She'd gone with the classic little black dress. Wide band sleeves rested just off her shoulders and flowed to a vee in front showing off a hint of cleavage. The material clung to her curves in a loose fit, allowing her to move. It was more provocative than sexy. And because Lexi liked sparkle and shine, the fabric glimmered with every step she took.

The automatic doors swooshed open to the glittering entrance of the casino. There were lights and movement everywhere. People, cars, taxies and valets flowed in a ballet of arrival and exits backlit by a cascading water feature.

A car waited for them and a valet rushed over to get the door. "Good evening, Mr. Calder, Lexi."

"Hi, Miguel, how's the new baby?"

A huge grin lit up his face. "As pretty as her mama."

"Miguel and his wife just had a baby girl a month ago," Lexi told Calder. "Her name is Saralynn."

There was no change to Calder's expression, but he nodded at Miguel. "Congratulations. Lexi," he gestured to the open door, "we have to get going."

"Of course."

Cold fish—check.

Strangely disappointed, she slid in and across the seat. When she glanced back, she saw Calder tip Miguel with a couple of hundred dollar bills. She perked up. Maybe not so cold after all. He joined her, his large body taking up most of the space. She suddenly felt crowded and overly warm. Definitely not cold now.

She might panic—if she were the type to panic—if he didn't smell so good. No fancy cologne for him. He smelled of soap and man. And he made her mouth water.

Rein it in, girl, you're on a mission here.

As a distraction, she focused on his generous gesture. It gave her a sense of hope. He'd stated in more than one article that he didn't want kids or a family, that he didn't have the patience or skill set for a long-term relationship so why set himself up for failure. Her plan rested on the fact he meant what he said, but it helped to know he wasn't totally dispassionate about kids. She needed him to care enough to act.

"How do you know Miguel?"

Jethro ground his teeth, annoyed he let the question slip out.

How she knew the other man didn't matter as long as she was a pretty armpiece and was able to intercede when required to redirect the conversation.

A task she should have no problem with since she'd been chattering ever since they met.

"Just from working at the Pinnacle. I've been at the spa now for a month. I like to talk to people so I've met a lot of the Pinnacle employees."

Yes, he could see her as a people person. Where he was not.

"Miguel treated his wife to a day at the spa after Saralynn was born. I thought it was a wonderful gesture and suggested to the owner that she put together a package just for new mothers and publicize it throughout the casino and hotel. She agreed to give it a try. We've had quite a few women come in."

"So you're in marketing?"

"Oh, goodness, no. I'm a dan—a hairdresser."

His head swung around and he rolled his gaze over her, accessing every curve. The escorts at Excursions were a mix of entertainers and professional businesswomen. He'd made it clear he preferred the latter. He had more in common with a businesswoman. And the one time he took a date to the next level had been with a dancer. He'd regretted the slip.

He preferred to keep his social and sexual encounters separate. He prized the discretion and privacy Excursions' services provided. He liked that sex wasn't part of the arrangement. The last thing he wanted was for the line between social and private to blur. That could only lead to complications and expectations he had no desire to deal with.

He never lacked for partners when he needed sexual release.

Casual dates with no promise of a follow-up were harder to come by until a friend recommended Excursions.

Having a new woman on his arm on a regular basis gave him the image of a player. He didn't care. He wasn't out to impress anyone and it gave warning to those who would expect more from him, all the better.

He'd made the mistake of sleeping with a date only once. She'd been a stunning woman of mixed race and he'd been out with her several times. Her intelligence and grace made him the envy of every man at the foundation dinner they'd attended. He'd been receiving an award and drank more than usual to offset the attention. Being in the limelight tore at his nerves but his date thrived on it. She'd been the perfect person to have on his arm that night and the high of the event had carried them upstairs when she made her interest clear.

Alliyah was gone in the morning and the next time he contacted Excursions he asked for a professional woman so he hadn't seen her again.

Excursions' quality control was slipping if they'd sent him a dancer. And he didn't even have her name beyond Miguel's addressing her as Lexi. He usually got notice and a new profile when he was getting a replacement date. He liked to know something about the women he spent time with even when he paid for the pleasure. He sent off a text.

"A dancer." He repeated.

"No. I told you, I work at Modern Goddess. I used to be a dancer." She licked her lips drawing his attention to the sultry lines of her mouth, the perfect bow over a plump bottom lip. "Now I do hair at the spa. I just thought pampering a new mother totally made sense. I remembered how tired and stressed my roommate was after having my goddaughter, Jasmine."

"Hmm. What's your name?"

"Oh, goodness." She laughed—an infectious sound that filled the back of the car. "We kind of skipped that part, didn't we? I'm Alexa Malone, but you can call me Lexi. And of course you're Jethro Calder. I read the article in the Pinnacle newsletter where it showed you and the other executives holding up the lifetime award of excellence for the Pinnacle game. That must have been exciting."

"Yes, it was a nice acknowledgment for the success of the game."

"I should say so. A top ten seller for ten years, that's awesome."

"It's actually been for fifteen years and more than half

those years it was in the top three, but they wanted to have wiggle room for future awards."

"What's it like working with Jackson Hawke?"

He frowned. He got that question a lot, mostly from people trying to angle through him to Jackson. But there was nothing in her tone or demeanor to indicate anything other than simple interest.

"He's a brilliant programmer, but he leaves the finances to me."

"Of course." She nodded and pointed at him.

She used her hands a lot when she talked. He couldn't decide if he found it charming or annoying. Whether he found her charming or was just attracted to that luscious mouth.

"We all have our talents, don't we? Mine is music. So, Jethro, where are we going?"

Music, he noticed, not dance.

"We're going to an event at Caesar's Palace." His phone buzzed and he read the text. "At least I am. I'm not sure what you'll be doing." He held up his phone. "Excursions doesn't have your name on file. Who are you?"

CHAPTER TWO

Oops. LEXI BLINKED at Jethro. She'd been caught out. She shifted her gaze to the phone he held aloft as evidence of her culpability and her eyes went wide.

The position of his arm caused his suit and shirtsleeves to slip down revealing his wrist and the tip of the birthmark. Enough for her to see it matched Jazi's.

The mark reminded Lexi of a dragonfly with a curled tail only kind of blotchy. She'd been stunned when she saw it on Calder's wrist in the picture accompanying the article she told him about. The top execs of Pinnacle had all been holding the award aloft. Calder had been standing closest to the camera and there on his wrist was the same birthmark as her precious Jazi's.

Lexi had known instantly that he had to be related to the baby, most likely her father. When she'd read his stance on never having a family, she firmly believed it was a sign. With his help she could get Jazi back.

Between the matching eyes and the birthmark, Lexi had all the confirmation she needed that Jethro Calder was Jazi's father.

"Ms. Malone?" Fingers snapped in front of her eyes.

She blinked and focused on the man next to her, staring into his unreadable features, into Jazi's blue eyes. Thoughts of how important he was flooded her mind, crippling her with fear. If she blew this she'd never get Jazi back! And she was about to blow it. Big-time.

Stop. Get a grip.

She drew in a slow, deep breath, released it around a

sheepish smile. She only had one option now. She looked him right in the eye and confessed. "I'm sorry. You're right, I don't usually work for Excursions."

A dark brow lifted at her easy admission. "So you were just at the restaurant to shanghai a date with me?"

"Oh, gracious, no." Now his other brow lifted. Had she offended him? She half shrugged. Best to stick as close to the truth as possible without getting Excursions in trouble. "Today was my best friend Alliyah's birthday. She used to go to work for Excursions. She passed away six months ago and I needed a distraction tonight, so I called Sally and asked if she could hook me up with a date. She said she had a cancellation and here I am."

"A cancellation?" Suspicion dripped from the question.

"Yes. You can call her if you like." Lexi held her breath—the last thing she wanted was to cause trouble for Sally.

"You recognized me."

"Yes, from the article. Why, did you know Alliyah? Alliyah West?"

He looked away, but nodded. "We had a couple of dates. You said she passed away."

"She was killed in an auto accident just over six months ago."

"I'm sorry to hear that. She was a charming companion."

Lexi glanced out the window and saw they were cruising along the dazzling Las Vegas Strip. "So listen, I'm sorry I'm not what you were expecting. You can let me out anywhere along here. I'll catch a cab back to the Pinnacle." She batted her eyelashes at him in an obvious ploy. "Unless you still need a date for the evening?"

"Now you're propositioning me?"

"No." She rolled her eyes and shook her head. "You know you can be a bit of a stuffed shirt. You might want to watch that. I'm offering—free of charge—to go with you to whatever thing you have going on so you don't have to find a replacement date."

"You're willing to spend the evening with a stuffed shirt?"

"Hey, I've been out with worse. At least you smell good and have a nice ride. But if you're not interested, just have the driver pull over and drop me off."

"Let's say I agree to allow you to accompany me, I'd prefer to pay you for your time."

Lexi blinked at him. "Why?"

"Because I prefer to keep our association on a professional level."

"You want me to cut your hair?" She said it just to rile him. The man had no sense of humor. Or sense of fun.

"What?" His brows drew together in a scowl. "Why would you suggest such a thing?"

"Because I'm a cosmetologist and my profession is to cut hair."

"That's not what I meant." His shoulders were razor sharp against the black leather seat. "More, you know it wasn't."

"You're right, I'm messing with you, but you deserve it for being so pompous."

"A stuffed shirt and now pompous," he muttered.

"They're nearly the same thing. And obviously your comfort zone."

"I merely wish to keep things clear."

"Oh, I get the point. It wouldn't be a date."

"That is correct. And as I value my time, I feel it only fair to pay you for yours."

"Very gracious of you."

He sighed and relaxed slightly.

"But forget it." She patted his knee and flashed a bright smile. "We'll just go as friends."

He practically choked on his own breath. "We are not friends. I barely know you."

"Sometimes people just click and are friends for life."

"There was no click."

"We even have a history." She talked right over him. "We both knew Alliyah, were friends of hers." If anyone needed a friend, it was this man. He was so cut off from everyone around him. For some reason, Lexi felt compelled to be there for him tonight. Perhaps because he was Jazi's father or maybe just because she hated to see anyone so alone. "Close enough, don't you think?"

His hand closed over hers on the seat. "You miss her very much don't you?"

Tears threatened. She nodded, and without thought turned her hand over in his to give his hand an answering squeeze. "It would be payment enough to spend the evening with someone who knew her."

"Then that's what we'll do." He pulled away from her. "As long as it's understood that it's not a date."

"Understood. There will be no good-night kiss."

He gave a shake of his head. "I may be a stuffed shirt, Ms. Malone, but you are outrageous."

"Huh. You say that like it's a bad thing."

He dropped his head forward as if he'd reached the end of his patience, but she thought she saw just the tiniest of smiles at the corner of his mouth.

"The event at Caesar's Palace is an art showing at the Maxim Gallery."

Interest flared in her bright blue eyes. "Oh, that sounds like fun. I've heard of the Maxim. I'll warn you, though, that I know nothing about art."

"There's no need for you to have knowledge of art." Jethro assured her.

He was still wondering at himself for allowing her to join him at the opening. It was unlike him to make impulsive decisions. And he didn't reward dishonesty. She may be from Excursions, but she was unlike any of his previous dates. And a former dancer. That alone should have been enough to drop her off along the strip as she'd urged him to do.

But there was a lightness about her that appealed to him, a genuineness that intrigued his jaded soul.

Outrageous was an understatement. No one talked to him like she did. Stuffed shirt? Pompous? He'd fire anyone who dared say such a thing. It didn't matter that it was the truth. That he worked hard to maintain a hand's distance from everyone around him. He wouldn't be disrespected.

Coming from her it rang of the truth, plainly spoken.

"Good. Because my art appreciation is limited to knowing what I like, which could be anything from a good Elvis painting to a portrait of an old woman smiling. And I never know if there's any importance attached to the piece."

"Well, it's highly doubtful there's any significance to a velvet Elvis painting."

Soft laughter trilled through the air. She nudged his shoulder with hers. "I know that much, silly. But he was a huge contributor to the music world and I like the colors. When I look at the painting, I like to think he found peace."

So did Jethro. Elvis was a favorite artist of his. One more thing linking him to this woman when the softness of her was already too dangerous. She didn't fit in either of the two categories he allowed in his life.

"So you don't believe he's living a secret life somewhere?"

"No." Sadness briefly dimmed the animation of her delicate features. "Much as I'd like to believe he's still with us, music was too much a part of his soul for him to stay undetected all these years. He'd have to perform, and if he performed he'd be found."

Disconcerted because he held the same belief, he went on the offensive.

"How old are you?" he asked derisively. "Twenty-three? Twenty-four? You're too young to be an Elvis fan."

"Please, great music transcends age. And I'm twenty-seven. Old enough to know my own mind."

Not as young as he'd feared—or should that be hoped?

Against his better judgment, he'd decided to indulge himself tonight and enjoy a bit of light company, but having a few elements that put her beyond his strict restrictions would be helpful.

"We're here." The car rolled to a smooth stop. Jethro pushed the door open and stepped out.

"Good evening, Mr. Calder." A valet immediately appeared to greet him. "Welcome back to Caesar's Palace."

"Thank you. We're here for the Kittrell showing."

"Very good, sir. We've had a steady stream of arrivals for the showing tonight."

"That's good to hear." Jethro tipped the young African American before extending a hand to assist Lexi from the car.

"Sean!" she exclaimed and gave the valet a warm hug. "I'm glad to see you're back in town. How is your mother?"

Sean shifted, uncomfortable under Jethro's stern regard, but the smile he turned on Lexi was full of warmth. "On her feet again. The knee surgery was just what she needed to get her pep back."

"I'm glad to hear it. She's too young to be sitting on the couch. You tell her I said hi."

"I will. And I want to hear what's going on with you." Sean discreetly nodded in Jethro's direction. "We'll talk soon."

"Yes, I'm off to view art." She glanced his way, and Jethro absorbed the impact of her laughing eyes. "See you soon." She bid her friend goodbye and made her way to his side.

He claimed her hand. "Do you know every valet in Las Vegas?"

"I know a lot. For all the tourists, Las Vegas is a small town. At least when it comes to the world of entertainers. Valeting is a common way to pick up extra money or pay the bills between jobs."

"I see."

"Is there a problem?"

"No."

"Something's bothering you," she insisted. "Does it upset you that I stopped to speak to them? Because it would be rude to ignore the fact I know them."

"It's their job to provide discrete service and fade into the background. I'm sure they respect the dynamics of the job."

"You're saying it's okay to be rude."

"I'm saying, they're working."

"So you're a snob."

He sighed. "I'm not a snob. I just like getting where I'm going without a lot of meaningless chitchat."

"It wasn't meaningless." She protested. "I was genuinely interested in how his mother was doing."

"That's not the point."

"Then what is the point?" She easily kept stride with him as he led her toward the famous Caesar shopping mall.

"The point is it's rude to be making a fuss over other men when you're out with a man."

"But we're not on a date." She reminded him with a tad more satisfaction than he cared for.

"We're together. That's what counts."

"So it's okay for me to be rude to them, but not to you?"

"Correct. No. Stop messing with me. You're giving me a headache."

She grinned, obviously pleased to be called on her teasing. "If you loosened up a bit, you wouldn't get headaches."

"Woman, you are a headache."

"Ah, you say the nicest things. Oh, it's the thunderstorm. I love this. Do we have time to watch?"

Without waiting for a response she skipped—yes, *skipped*—forward to perch on the stone bench of a fountain. He found himself following her, taking satisfaction in indulging her delight. She patted the space next to her inviting him to sit.

Suddenly an uncertain expression crossed her face and

she popped to her feet. "Sorry—my *oops*. I know you want to get where you're going."

"Sit. Enjoy your show." He sat. "And when we get to the showing, you can do something for me."

"Ah." She resumed her perch, her knee touching his, her gaze focused above on the changing skyscape of the indoor mall. The sunny day had darkened to gray clouds with flashes of lightning. "The job your dates perform for you."

The comment annoyed him. So what if he wanted his companions to provide a service while they were with him. He paid good money for their company. And tipped well.

"You really are a pest. If you don't want to do it, you don't have to."

"Don't be so touchy." She bumped his shoulder. "Ah." A gasp escaped her pretty lips when thunder boomed in the background adding audio to the overhead show. "I do love a good thunderstorm. I don't get how all these people can walk by as if nothing is happening right over their heads."

"Maybe they've seen it before. Or they're caught up in the moment or the conversation. Or simply need to be somewhere." Personally he couldn't remember the last time he'd paused to notice the movement of the mock sky in the shopping mall. He had to admit it was pretty cool. It certainly added to the overall effect of a Roman city.

"What have you got?"

"I'm thinking this might be something to consider for Pinnacle for our next revamp. We could have simulated battle scenes."

"Oh, and flames like the city is burning. With the postapocalyptic theme you could do all kinds of things with the skyscape, extreme sunsets and meteor storms, flash floods. You could even bring it down on the walls though that might compete with the casino action."

"The tourists would love it. It would give them the sense of being in the game even more than the decor does now."

He liked the creative way she thought. All tossed out so

artlessly. Right. In his experience, nothing, not even ideas, were given away free. She wanted something.

He'd bet his life on it.

Above them, blue skies began to ease out the clouds and lightning. Lexi stood and smoothed her dress over her hips.

"It's a great idea, but what I was actually asking is what would you like me to do for you at the party?"

CHAPTER THREE

PARTY? BLAST IT. In order to get his mind functioning again, Jethro dragged his gaze up to her face, not daring to linger on the intriguing hint of cleavage or her luscious lower lip.

She meant the showing. He'd almost lost his desire to attend the event tonight. But as owner of the gallery and the artist's patron it would look bad if he didn't at least put in an appearance. Plus, he believed in the man's talent.

He and his friends made a great team evidenced by their huge success with Pinnacle. Yet the last few years, he'd felt compelled to prove he could succeed on his own. The gallery, like the restaurant, was his attempt at diversification.

"It's nothing too difficult." He stood, his hand going to the small of her back as he directed her along. "As a high-ranking officer at one of the premier entertainment conglomerates in the world, I get approached by a lot of people with ideas for the next best whatever. I'd like you to run interference for me."

"I can see where that would get old." Sympathy shone from eyes the color of the pastoral sky above. "Sure, I can handle that. Tell me about the artist."

"He takes parts of photographs, layers them together and breathes life into them with an editing software he created. The end result is stunning, the colors vivid."

"I can't wait to see his work. It sounds unlike anything I've ever seen."

Jethro must be impressed with the artist. Talking about him was the most animated she'd seen him all night. Though, to be fair, he had loosened up from his stuffed-shirt status by allowing her to watch the sky show and by sharing his thoughts about revamping the Pinnacle.

At the gallery the crowd overflowed into the mall.

"Well, I'd say the showing is a success." Lexi wrapped her arm around Jethro's to keep from being separated from him. "And it's such a crush nobody's going to hear anyone in here. I don't think you need to worry about being approached by any wannabe gamesters."

He grunted. "You underestimate the zealousness of programmers, songwriters and other assorted artists the world over. A crowd like this just allows them the opportunity to get up close and personal."

Actually she knew full well the zealousness of artists. No one knew better than her how one-dimensional they could be when it came to their art.

"Maybe it's your warm personality," she suggested.

She grinned when she received an arch stare over his shoulder. "You like to live dangerously don't you?"

"Sorry. I can't seem to resist." And she should. Her every action counted toward the future and his willingness to help her. But she'd been restrained for too many years not to be herself at all times. Plus, who knew he'd be so fun to tease? Or turn out to be such a good sport? "Take heart, you're bearing up under the challenge."

Right inside the door hung a huge picture that was gorgeous. A tropical location brought to life in vibrant colors. The nose of a small plane bobbed in the cove and on the beach a gazebo with fluttering curtains housed a table, chairs and a meal awaiting missing lovers. To the side of the print were a picture of a lagoon, the plane and a gazebo. The title was *Escape*.

"I love it," Lexi breathed. "Don't you just want to be there?"

"It's inviting."

"Inviting? If that's all you've got, I'm going to have to find someone else to go with."

"Someone with a sense of adventure," a man said behind her.

"Yes." She agreed, moving to include the tall, stylishly dressed man. He had long dark hair, green eyes and a confidence he wore as comfortably as his fitted jacket. "And a sense of romance. Someone with a thirst for life."

"Exactly the mood I was going for." The man grinned and held out his hand. "I'm Ethan Kittrell."

"Ethan is the artist." Jethro shook hands as he introduced Lexi.

"Calder, I'm glad you made it. And for bringing such a lovely companion."

"Are you flirting with my companion, Ethan?" There was no emotion in the question, which only served to make it more menacing.

As if she belonged to him. Not likely. She'd fought hard for her freedom. And wasn't he the one to insist this wasn't a date?

But truthfully she wasn't even tempted by the handsome artist. For all his eccentric cleverness, he paled next to the sheer presence of Jethro Calder.

Good thing this wasn't a date. Because, her independence aside, she'd be way out of her element.

No, tonight was make-believe, just an opportunity to observe him in his world. Which meant she could be herself. As long as she didn't alienate him, she could relax and have fun.

"Not tonight, I'm not." Ethan held up his hands in surrender and shifted ever so subtly away from her. "Just a little harmless admiration for a beautiful woman. I wouldn't want to do anything to upset my patron."

"Wise move." Jethro directed her farther into the gallery, pausing to study each new piece they came to.

Patron? No wonder he'd been hot to get here. A patron to the arts, hmm, seemed there were unexpected depths to Mr. Jethro Calder. Still, being a patron was no excuse to be rude.

"Pay no attention to him." She rolled her eyes at Ethan. "He's still learning his people skills."

"Sweet thing, people use skills on him not the other way around."

"So he tells me." She surveyed Jethro's profile, and observed the pinch at the corner of his eye, a sure sign he hated them talking about him. This was a big night for him as well as Ethan. "He practically gushed while describing your work."

"I have never gushed in my life."

"You were quite animated. With good reason. I love, love, love these pieces." She leaned in close to a picture of an old firehouse with a clock tower. Beside it were photos of a barn, a fire truck and a watch with exposed gears. "Is it a stippling effect?"

"Very perceptive. I'm a master of shadows."

"Really? Shadows." She stepped back and looked at the picture again.

A hand at her waist drew her in front of Jethro. He followed the line of the fire truck with his finger. "The shadows disguise the layering and add depth and dimension." He spoke right in her ear, his breath blowing over the sensitive skin. She shivered and fought the urge to lean back against him.

"Yes. I can see the shadows are key."

"Ethan, there you are. And Jethro, you finally made it. Excellent." A woman with pale skin, black sharp-edged hair and bright red lips swept up to them. She wore a black suit that flowed around a reed-thin body. Hooking her arms through each of the men's, she led them away. "The press are here. Time to make nice."

Lexi followed as best she could considering the crowd quickly closed around her now she didn't have the almighty Jethro Calder with her. When she got cut off, she decided to look around at more of the art. The woman obviously worked for the gallery and it sounded like Jethro would be busy for a few minutes, so he shouldn't miss her.

As she strolled around, she encountered several people she knew. The director of her last dance review at the Golden Link and his wife, a pit boss from Pinnacle and his partner, and a client of hers from Modern Goddess. She chatted briefly with each making sure to talk up the artist; she even influenced a sale with the director.

She kept her eye on Jethro in case her duties were needed but the dark-haired woman, whom she'd learned was Lana, the gallery manager, guarded him like a lioness with her cub. No wannabes were getting through her.

Ethan found Lexi by the buffet table.

"Hey, I've been racking up sales for you."

"I'm glad to hear it." He grabbed one of the fancy bottles of water. "And I'm glad I caught you alone."

"Ah-ah." She shook her finger at him. "You promised Jethro no flirting."

"He's who I want to talk to you about. I want to thank him for his patronage by giving him one of the pictures. I thought you could help me choose one for him."

"Oh, goodness. We really haven't known each other that long."

"Maybe not, but you obviously have his number. And he likes you."

What an interesting comment. She wondered what made him think so. She laughed. "I think we both have you fooled."

"No." Ethan shook his head, his green gaze serious. "As a photographer and an artist, I've learned to read people. I'll admit Jethro is tough to get a read on because he doesn't show much emotion. Most people don't even try unless they want something from him."

"That's just sad." She dismissed a pang of guilt. He couldn't miss what he didn't know he had.

"Yes." Ethan sipped the expensive water. "But it's a persona he fosters. He doesn't let people close."

"You're just proving my case."

"I'm proving my case. Because *you* see the man. You recognized his excitement for my work. You tease him." He shook his head. "Seriously, I've never seen anyone talk to him the way you do. And he takes it. That's how I know he likes you."

Okay, he'd made a couple of good points, but Lexi still wasn't convinced. She'd love for Jethro to like her. It could only help her case, make him predisposed to help her. But the evidence seemed pretty flimsy to her.

"That and the way he looks at you. He hasn't taken his eyes off you all night."

Of course the comment had her searching out Jethro, and sure enough he looked right at them even as he talked with an elderly Japanese couple. She waved and he cocked a dark brow.

"This should really be your choice." She told Ethan.

"I'd still like your help." He insisted.

"Okay, but I should get back to him soon."

"This won't take long," he assured her. "And he's busy taking care of business so we have time."

"Business? You mean patron stuff?"

"No. He doesn't have to do much with that except praise my work."

Uh-oh. She sought him out again. Had she misread the Japanese couple? Could they be overeager gamesters she should be saving him from?

"He's dealing with boring owner stuff." Taking her arm Ethan led her to the first picture. It already had a red dot indicating it had been sold. "There's plenty of time for you to help me."

"I didn't know Jethro owned the gallery. Is he going to be moving it to the Pinnacle?"

"He hasn't mentioned any plans to do so. And it has a following here, so I wouldn't think so."

Interesting. Calder was associated so closely with Pinnacle, she found it difficult to think of him branching out to other casinos. But then Pinnacle wasn't just a casino but part of a huge entertainment conglomerate. The company started out creating and distributing video games. The hotel and casino were decorated based off the first game, a postapocalyptic world where everyone fought to survive.

The diversification made her wonder if he might be considering breaking away from Pinnacle. When she got the time, she'd have to think of what that might mean to her plans.

"Has Jethro shown an interest in any particular piece?" she asked Ethan. "That might be a place to start."

"Good idea. Let me think." He stopped and propped his hands on his hips. His gaze ran over his work displayed on the walls. "No. He's shown general appreciation but not for any specific piece. As I said, Jethro doesn't give up a lot about himself. That's why I was hoping you could help."

Lexi spied a picture of a smoking cigar in a crystal ashtray next to a bottle of aged bourbon in the forefront of an old-fashioned parlor. The colors were muted but powerful. She thought of the old-world elegance of Jethro's restaurant and knew he would appreciate the piece.

"That one." She nodded toward the painting. "It would fit nicely in his restaurant so it's something he'll like."

Ethan considered the painting and then nodded. "You're right. It fits him. Let me grab it before someone buys it. Thanks." He dropped a kiss on her head and strolled off.

"He's still making moves on my date," Jethro drawled close to her ear. "I might have to have a talk with him."

Lexi jumped and swirled around. "Geez, how long have you been there?"

"I just walked up. Why? Something happen you don't want me to know about?"

"Nope. You startled me, is all." Looking to divert his attention from Ethan, she gestured to the crowd. "You must be pleased. Ethan told me you own the gallery."

"It's a recent acquisition."

"Calder." Her former director and his wife came up to them. They made a stunning older couple. "You're doing a great job here at the gallery. Ethan Kittrell is quite a find."

"Thomas and Irene." Jethro offered his hand to the couple. "Thanks for coming. We're always pleased to provide something unique for our collectors."

"Indeed. Irene fell in love with a couple of prints we'll be taking off your hands."

"Irene, I've always admired your taste."

The older woman beamed under his approval. "And you've redeemed my opinion of yours when it comes to women. Oh, I know how you young men like to play the field, but I hope you realize what a treasure you have in this girl."

"You know Lexi." Jethro's expression went blank.

Oops. Time to do her job. He was either insulted, and trying to find a nice way to tell a good client to mind her own business. Or counting to ten before blasting her, with no consideration of future relations.

"Irene, you're going to make me blush." Lexi interceded before Jethro could react. "There's actually nothing romantic going on. Jethro knew Alliyah and today was her birthday. We're just celebrating her together this evening." She smiled through the sadness. "She would have loved this."

"Oh, my dear." Sympathy filled Irene's brown eyes. "She would indeed. My apologies, Jethro. Such a tragedy to lose her so young. Do you know how her—"

"Family is doing?" Lexi quickly interrupted before Irene could mention Alliyah had a daughter. "Yes. Everyone misses Alliyah terribly but we're doing as well as can be expected."

"Good, that's good. She's lucky to have had you for a friend. You let us know if we can do anything."

"Absolutely," Thomas confirmed. "And remember, you're welcome back with the troupe anytime you want."

"Thank you both. You have a good evening now." She gave them both a peck on the cheek and sent them on their way.

"Sorry about that." She patted Jethro on the arm. "But no harm done."

She hoped not anyway. She wanted to be the one to tell Jethro about Jazi. To gauge his reaction and sway him to her cause. He was a sharp guy; she didn't want him to be wondering about a child in Alliyah's life and start counting down the months.

"What are you after?"

"What?"

Jethro's firm grip on her arm gave her no option but to join him in a dimly lit hallway.

"Hey." She tried to shake her arm loose, but he held on.

"Who are you?" he demanded.

"I don't know what you mean. I'm Lexi."

"How is it that you know everyone?"

"I don't know everyone. That's crazy." She pulled against his grip. "You're hurting me." Not really, but he had her unnerved and that was close enough.

"Quit squirming and it won't hurt." His fingers loosened but he retained his hold, forcing her to follow him down the hall.

"Let me go and I'll quit squirming."

He opened the door of a well-appointed office. It had a feminine feel and Lexi guessed it belonged to Lana, the gallery manager.

Jaw clenched, he released her. Then frowned at the red marks on her skin. "Your skin is too delicate."

She rubbed her arm singeing him with a reproachful glare. "Apology accepted."

She dropped into a visitor's chair and crossed her legs.

"Sorry," he muttered belatedly, grudgingly. He sat on the edge of the desk. "Now tell me how you know so many people. I saw you talking with people all over the gallery."

"Just because I talked to people doesn't mean I know them. Is this about me not protecting you from the madding crowd? You seemed fine whenever I glanced your way."

"Mocking me will not save you. Answer the question."

"Save me?" She laughed.

He didn't.

"You targeted me, Ms. Malone. I want to know why."

CHAPTER FOUR

LEXI PUSHED THROUGH her front door, slammed it shut behind her and threw the bolts. Unable to shake the sense of being pursued, she backed away.

Pull it together, girl. The man had better things to do than chase her down.

After Jethro dropped his question bomb, she'd slipped out when Lana and Ethan walked in carrying the piece Ethan had chosen for Jethro.

Best timing ever.

Okay, she'd panicked.

She hadn't been prepared for his questions.

In the bedroom she grabbed a nightgown—a lavender bit of silk edged in black lace—and headed into the bathroom for a shower. She'd bolted. What else could she do? He thought she was some femme fatale intent on getting something from him.

And, in a way, she was.

He'd been so intense she didn't know if she'd ever be prepared to face off against him.

But she would. For Jazi.

Lexi clung to the fact he gave Miguel a healthy tip when he learned of his new baby. It showed he had some sensitivity for kids. Right?

During the cab ride home she'd decided she needed to call tomorrow and make an appointment with Jethro. She'd see him before she went into work and get this all straightened out.

Stepping under the spray, she rinsed her hair, letting the

hot water soothe her. As plans went, it lacked finesse and relied heavily on his willingness to see her again. But what she'd learned of him tonight told her an up-front, honest approach was her best bet.

All the things she could say filtered through her head as she dried off and applied a tropical-scented lotion in honor of Ethan's *Escape* painting. The silk of her nightgown glided over her skin in a sensual fall, ending at midthigh. She continued to ruminate while combing and drying her hair. The thick auburn tresses were still damp when she thought she heard a knock on her door.

Flipping off the hairdryer, she listened and the knocking came again. She wrinkled her nose. The last thing she needed tonight was the distraction of a friend coming over for gossip and coffee, something dancers liked to do. Since she'd left the troupe, she often had people dropping by.

Or maybe that's exactly what she needed. To just get out of her head and focus on someone else for a while. By the time she reached the door, she was ready to embrace whoever stood on the other side.

She swung the door wide. "Hell…"

Bug-eyed, she stared at Jethro Calder.

"What? How?"

His navy eyes swept over her darkening to near black by the time his gaze met hers. Who knew black could show such heat? He stepped forward, crowding her.

Instinctively she backed away.

He kept coming and she kept retreating until he cleared the threshold. He closed the door behind him.

"Are you crazy?" he demanded. "You don't answer the door without knowing who's on the other side." His gaze made another journey over her as he continued to stalk her. "Especially dressed like that.

"How are you here?" She meant it as an accusation. It came out in a whisper as she continued to dodge his pursuit. She hit a chair and sidestepped.

"Does it matter?" He caught her elbow when she tripped over the ottoman and nearly landed on her rump. "You wanted me and, sunshine, you've got me." Lifting her to her toes, he lowered his head and slanted his lips over hers.

Her hands landed on his chest ready to push him away. But oh, my...

For all his ferocity, when his mouth took hers, there was no anger, no punishing assault on her senses, nothing but pure passion, undiluted desire. The soft pressure of his lips lured her into opening to him.

Oh, he took, with a seductive demand that had her lifting farther onto her toes and looping her arms around his neck. Her mind was lost, transferring the cadence of his touch to notes in her head. Grip, glide, soft, firm, thrust, nip—the heat built in body and melody to a place she'd never been before.

He whispered erotic threats and words were added to the song in her head.

As she floated on sensation, he became her rock, hard, solid, grounded. His arms were a haven of safety and the orchestrators of the sensation and rhythm surging through her.

She wanted more. Now. More of his taste, more of his touch, more of his heat. More.

And then her knees hit up against something and she sat. She blinked and her bedroom came into focus. He'd moved them down the hall and into her room without her even noticing they were moving.

Eyes liquid with arousal, he watched her as he unbuttoned his shirt. He'd lost his jacket somewhere along the trek to the bedroom.

And OMG, she'd lost her nightgown. She sat in front of him in nothing more than a rosy blush of need.

Sanity came rushing back with a roar.

"Stop. Whoa." Grabbing the edge of her sunny yellow comforter, she wrapped it around herself. She wasn't modest, a dancer couldn't afford the luxury, but she felt too exposed under his ravenous regard. "I'm sorry, but this is not going to happen."

His fingers froze on the last connected button. "Excuse me?" Dark brows lowered in a fierce scowl.

Intimidating, much? Oh, yeah.

"I'm sorry," she said again. And she meant it. He'd just lit her up like a torch in every way imaginable, body, mind, soul. And he couldn't be more off-limits if he were the Pope. "This isn't what I intended when I sought you out."

If anything the scowl deepened. "Explain."

The demand was nearly a growl. It occurred to her she should be afraid, but she wasn't. She'd been in his arms, felt his body resonate with hers. He'd never hurt a woman. Not physically anyway. He had too much control. But there were worse ways he could make her pay. Her mind raced. This needed to be handled carefully.

Feeling at a disadvantage, she inched to the side and stood up. He stepped back giving her some room. She breathed in relief. "I'd prefer to get dressed for this conversation if you don't mind."

It wasn't a question and still he looked ready to protest, a signal to her that he was in charge of what happened here. Never mind it was her apartment. Clearly the man was used to being in command wherever he went. Finally, he gave a brief nod and left the room.

Okay, in no way did his silence reassure her. Anger defined the rigid line of his shoulders as he strode away.

"There's wine in the refrigerator and glasses in the cupboard to the right," she called out, then bit her lip. This wasn't a date, but she knew if he left, she'd lose all chance of ever talking to him.

Ready or not the time had come to plead her case.

She grabbed clothes from the dresser and hurried into them, soft gray sweats and a baby-blue sweater cropped at the waist. In the bathroom she tamed her hair into a ponytail and noticed the pants clung to the curves of her butt and the sweater played peekaboo with her belly button. Dang. Time didn't allow for another change.

Tugging at the hem of the sweater she went to wrangle the shark in her living room.

He leaned against the counter of her kitchen island, sipping a glass of wine. His dark gaze ran over her making her senses tingle.

"You have five minutes," he stated in that near growl that just added to his effect on her body.

Ignoring the urges she could never act on, she helped herself to some wine. She perched on one of the bar stools at the island and took a sip.

"Four minutes. Don't try my patience, Ms. Malone."

"I really wanted to do this differently. I was going to come by your office—" She slanted him a wry glance and reached for a picture frame at the end of the counter. Handing it to him, she said softly, "Alliyah had a daughter. Her name is Jasmine. She's twenty-three-months-old."

He refused to accept the picture, didn't even glance at it. "What does that have to do with me?"

"You said I targeted you. This is why. In the article I read about Pinnacle, there was a picture included. You and the other executives were holding up the award. I saw your birthmark."

One dark brow lifted. "You targeted me because of my birthmark?"

So cool, so unaffected when her whole life weighed in the balance.

"Yes." She hesitated, prayed this was the right decision, that she wasn't risking losing Jazi to the one person Lexi could never get her back from. "Because Jasmine has the same birthmark."

Okay, she had Jethro's attention. Truthfully, she'd had his attention from the moment she walked into The Beacon in that snug little black dress and he hoped she'd be his date. But never in his wildest imaginings had he considered the night would end up here. He'd been suspicious of her, enough to follow her here.

The sight of her draped in damp silk, white teeth biting her lush lower lip, had sidetracked him for an irrational moment. A hot, blow-his-mind moment that should never have happened. The lack of discipline was in no small part responsible for his...mood.

No one ever accused him of being dense. She meant to suggest Jasmine was his daughter. And he dealt with numbers every day, so he could do the math. The timing fit. But not the circumstances. He never had unprotected sex, never.

"Coincidence," he stated.

She groaned and shook her head. "You don't strike me as a man big on coincidence."

She wasn't wrong. But he didn't budge. No way was she laying this on him. Family wasn't in his future. In order to survive, he'd had to shut down his emotions. It was a lesson too well learned to change. Plus, he'd force no one to share his secret shame. All in all he sucked at relationships, lacked the skill set as one woman told him. When he hit thirty, he quit trying. He'd found Excursions about a year later.

So no, no family for him. And he was fine with that. He'd come to terms with the notion long ago, had made it clear to all who knew him. Jethro wasn't prepared for that to change now.

Certainly not on the whim of a woman he barely knew. Even if she turned him so upside down he'd practically jumped her as soon as he'd walked inside the door. What had he been thinking?

The problem was he hadn't been thinking; he'd been feeling. Further proof emotions couldn't be trusted.

"You have the wrong man."

Lexi slid from the stool and held the picture frame up in front of him. "She has your eyes."

Don't look. It's a ploy. She just wants a rich baby daddy to support the orphan and you're the lucky dupe.

The warning blasted through Jethro's brain. But not even his legendary restraint proved stronger than the compulsion to look.

The baby was beautiful. A little girl with wild black curls and a smile so big and sweet he felt blessed just seeing it. She danced in the picture, her arms were raised and her tiny butt was cocked to the side and one pink-sandaled foot poised in the air. Jethro spied a smudge on one wrist that could be a birthmark. She had light beige skin, a sharp little nose.

And midnight-blue eyes ringed by lush black lashes.

Yeah, the birthmark was iffy, but those eyes, he'd never seen that exact color anywhere but in the mirror. The shape of her eyes, and her straight little eyebrows also matched his.

"I'm not looking for money." Lexi broke the silence. "And I don't expect you to change your life. I read that you don't want a family."

"Then what is this about, Ms. Malone?" He placed the picture facedown on the counter, the better to concentrate on the woman before him. His life just did a one-eighty. He needed to focus. "What do you want?"

"Can you call me Lexi?" Her cheeks flushed a delightful shade of pink. "We just shared…" She waved her hand in the direction of the bedroom. "…a moment. It seems foolish to be so formal."

"I've been foolish in more than one regard tonight, Ms. Malone—calling me on it isn't your smartest move."

"Why foolish?" she demanded, crossing her arms over her chest.

Her position drew attention to her breasts, which were small but plump. And pert, a detail he remembered in vivid Technicolor. Her stance also caused a thin strip of pale skin to show at her waist. His fingers itched to touch that silky skin again.

"Because you didn't have control of every moment of

the evening?" she went on. "Because you actually enjoyed yourself? News flash, people do it all the time."

"Because none of it was real." Or did her show of attitude indicate otherwise? Was she upset because she, too, had got more caught up in their time together than she'd intended?

So what if she was? It didn't matter. Couldn't matter. She was so off-limits she may as well live on Venus.

"What do you want from me?" If it wasn't money or for him to assume care of Jasmine, which would definitely change his life, then what else was there?

She sighed and relaxed her stance. "I want to adopt her."

He lifted both brows. That was a response he hadn't expected. And why did it give him mixed feelings of relief and disappointment?

"Sounds like you have it all worked out. So why do you need me?"

A look of anguish flashed through her pure blue eyes.

"Even though I'm Jazi's godmother and it's what Alliyah would want, I don't meet the qualifications for an adoptive parent. I'm single and a dancer." She shrugged as if that said it all. "I need you to assume custody and then we can do a private adoption."

Custody. The word sent a rumble of dread down his back. And made him wonder. "Where is she?"

"Child Protective Services took her away. She's in foster c-care." She pressed her lips together and blinked a couple of times. "Alliyah would hate that."

The thought of his daughter in foster care burned like acid through his blood.

Except she may not be his daughter at all. The fact she had a birthmark and his eyes was circumstantial at best. Still, he'd spent too many years in the grueling system to be placid about any innocent being tossed to that merciless grist mill.

"I get to see her and I go as often as they'll let me, but if I don't do something soon, they'll release her for adoption and I'll never get to see her again." In her eagerness, she stepped closer bringing the scent of a tropical night with her. She raised pleading eyes to his. "You have to help me."

"I don't actually." Time to go. This woman got to him. Had since the moment she walked into his world. If he didn't leave now, he'd promise her the moon. "I need to consider what you've told me." He moved to the door, grabbing his jacket en route. "I'll have my assistant call you for an appointment in the next day or two."

She nodded. Her arms were crossed over her chest again, but the pose held elements of disappointment and hope, as if she were holding herself together by a thread.

Damn it. He charged across the room and grabbed up the picture. "I'm taking this with me."

This time when he left, he didn't look back.

There was no going to sleep after Jethro's visit. She tried. And failed. She tossed and turned, replaying her conversation with him over and over in her head. After two hours, she finally gave up and crawled out of bed still not knowing what to think.

She dragged herself to the kitchen and the coffeepot. The scent of the fresh-ground beans perked her up. She stood over the machine as it brewed, holding her cup under the spigot to catch the first stream and then switching in the pot.

She wandered to the couch and curled up with her cup. Dancers by trade tended to be night people. She used to be at her peak at this hour. Tonight her brain barely functioned except it wouldn't shut off.

Jethro had pointed out he didn't have to help her. But he'd taken the picture. And his assistant would be calling to make an appointment. Did that mean he believed her? Or was his comment just a way to get him out of the apartment without a further scene and she'd never see him again?

No. She refused to believe he'd just walk away. She'd

seen the look in his eyes when he'd stared at the picture of Jazi. He saw the resemblance. And he'd act on it.

Wouldn't he?

Stop. She couldn't take this vicious Ferris wheel any longer. She drained her coffee and went to change. She needed to dance.

She'd given up her vocation, but she'd always dance. She needed the release like she needed to breathe. Especially now. The exercise would help her to get out of her head and relieve the tension still lingering in her body from its encounter with Jethro's. There had to be a gym open somewhere at this hour.

Jethro stood staring out the floor-to-ceiling window of his penthouse suite. The lights and flash of the Las Vegas Strip spread out before him in a glimmering kaleidoscope of color and movement. And he saw none of it.

He couldn't get the picture of a dancing baby with midnight-blue eyes out of his head.

He'd resolved to never have a family. But Lexi's announcement shook him. If he had a daughter, that changed everything.

Except it didn't have to.

Lexi wanted to raise the baby as her own. She couldn't be more clear that he wasn't invited to the party. His money and presence were not needed.

A knock came at the door and then Clay Hoffman stepped inside. Tall and blond, the man moved with military precision. You could put the grunt in a suit, but you couldn't take the army out of the man. A foster brother and friend, Clay ran all things security related for Pinnacle Enterprises.

"I got your summons." Clay went to the bar and helped himself to a drink. "What's the emergency?" He dropped down on the brown suede couch and glanced around. "Where are Jackson and Ryan?"

"They aren't coming." Jethro joined his friend in the living area. "This is personal."

"Personal?" Clay's brows rose. "And it couldn't wait until morning? Do you have an incident with one of your other companies? Cause you know the guys are more than willing to help even when it's not Pinnacle business."

"I prefer to keep this private for now." Jethro picked up his abandoned drink and sipped. The burn of whiskey down his throat—just what he needed to loosen his tongue. "It appears I may have a daughter."

"As if." Clay laughed and sipped his drink. "Come on, tell me what this is about."

Jethro simply stared at him.

Finally Clay's eyes went big and he shook his head. "You're serious. You have a daughter?"

"Maybe. Probably." Jethro glanced at the picture frame on the coffee table.

"Is this her?" Clay reached for the picture and stared. "Oh, hell."

"So you see it, too?"

"That she has your eyes? It's hard to miss."

"I'm told she has my birthmark, too."

Clay returned his attention to the photo and squinted. "Hmm. Could be, I guess. I'd want to see it up close to confirm. And we'll need a DNA test. Who is the mother?"

"And that's why I called you." He rarely asked for help. But in this case he knew his friend would direct him through the quagmire discreetly and efficiently. Jethro filled Clay in on all the details. "I need to know for certain she's mine before I make any decisions."

"Of course. I already have a sample of your DNA." The Fabulous Four were all millionaires and after Jackson went AWOL last year Clay had collected DNA samples from each of them as a security measure. "It shouldn't be a problem getting the baby's from the county. And I have a lab that will turn the results around in a day."

"Good." Jethro stood to pace. "I want to see her."

"Whoa." Clay held his hands up in a time-out gesture. "If you're serious about giving her up, that may not be a good idea."

"It's the right thing to do, don't you think? Giving her up?"

"Only you can answer that, bro." Clay's alert gaze pierced through Jethro's ambivalence. "You never talk about family, except to say you never planned to have one of your own."

"Because I don't have any. The foster system was never able to locate any next of kin for me." There was no record of who'd abandoned him. Kind of hard to get info from no one.

"In that case this little girl may be the only family you'll ever know. You should think carefully before you sign your rights away."

Jethro shot his friend a get-real grimace. "I'm not equipped to raise a kid. I don't scare easy but the thought of taking on custody of a little girl outright terrifies me. But I'd castrate myself before I left her in foster care."

"Ouch," Clay flinched, "but I hear you. You know it doesn't have to be all or nothing. You can negotiate the terms."

Jethro shook his head. Sharing custody with the red-hot redhead was not going to happen. Between baby and dancer, he'd never know another moment of peace. "Lexi made her terms clear. I won't jeopardize Jasmine's future."

He hesitated. "Jackson and Grace might raise her."

Jethro had considered the option, but he wouldn't do that to his friend. "They aren't even married yet. I can't ask them to do that. And if she were that close, I may not be able to refrain from interfering, which wouldn't be fair to anyone. No, Lexi Malone is her godmother. She obviously loves the child. It's the best solution."

"Then I recommend you don't see her."

Knowing Clay was right, Jethro struggled with the irrational compulsion. He prided himself on making dispassionate decisions. Not this time. "If she's mine, I have to see her."

Clay sighed. "If she's yours, I'll set it up."

Lexi's day didn't get any better as it wore on. Jethro's assistant called but the appointment had been postponed for a day.

The delay was torture. Every minute dragged. And what filled her head? The feel and taste of Jethro Calder. When she'd sought him out last night, the last thing she'd contemplated was an attraction to the man.

Because it complicated much?

Of course she never could have predicted he'd track her to her apartment and seduce her in her own living room. Thank her lucky stars she came to her senses before he actually got her in bed. But it had been too close, the struggle too hard for her peace of mind.

She hadn't lost her head like that in…no, she'd never lost her head like that. Been so swept away by a man's kiss, by his touch, that she lost all sense of the here and now.

The fact he was her goddaughter's father put him off-limits. Those forbidden moments in his arms were hot enough to give her regrets, but Jazi had to come first.

Desperate and longing to see her little girl, she called Jazi's foster mother about setting up an appointment to see the baby, but it wasn't convenient today. Instead they made arrangements for the next day.

Waiting proved too brutal so Lexi called in to Modern Goddess to see if she could put in extra hours and went into work early.

Between waiting and fighting off memories of Jethro's kiss it looked set to be a long day.

Long didn't describe her day. Try excruciating. Lexi decided she required the distraction of people around her for dinner. She didn't set out for that place to be The Beacon, but somehow that's where she ended up.

And surprise, surprise Calder sat at the bar.

Lexi hesitated, about to leave. They had an appointment for the next day. She should leave him in peace. Instead she slid onto the stool next to his.

"A glass of white wine, please," she said to the bartender. "Mr. Calder."

"Ms. Malone."

"Was your day a living hell? Because mine was."

"This is Las Vegas. It's not unusual for the weather to be warm this time of year."

She laughed. "And here I thought you had no sense of humor."

"I'd like a bit of peace with my drink if you don't mind."

"I do mind. I'm no good at waiting. I need someone to talk to and as I'm trying to be discreet about this whole thing, you're the only one I can talk to."

"You're assuming a lot."

"Not so much." Her wine appeared in front of her. She smiled her thanks at the bartender. "Our appointment tomorrow tells me you acted on the information I gave you."

"I may just want more information."

"If that were the case, the appointment would have been for today. You don't appear to be too good at waiting either."

He sent her a searing sideways glare. "The test results aren't back yet."

"Bummer." She sipped her wine. "I guess we'll have to talk about something else."

"Or you could go away."

"I just got my wine."

He tilted his drink, ice clinking against the glass. "I suppose next you'll want dinner."

"I thought you'd never ask." She snagged a pretzel from a bowl on the bar. "It'll be our second nondate."

"Is that supposed to be funny?" he demanded, clearly annoyed. "Because it's not funny."

"Ah, the stuffed shirt is back. Now he has no sense of humor."

He lifted a finger and the bartender came over. "Sam, a table for two please."

"Of course." Sam went back to serving.

In less than a minute the maître d' appeared beside them. "Sir, your table is ready."

"Thank you." Jethro gestured for her to follow the tall man.

"Do you like salmon?" he asked as they wound through the tables.

"I do."

The maître d' stopped and waved them into a quiet alcove where a large table was set for two. "Is there anything I can get for you?"

"Two specials. Would you care for another drink?" Jethro addressed the question to her.

"No, but I'd like water, please." She unfolded the linen napkin into her lap.

Jethro nodded to the maître d'. The man bowed and acknowledged, "Two specials and two waters. Enjoy your meal."

"Nice." The alcove had the feel of an elegant library with a faux fireplace. Above the mantel Lexi admired the Kittrell picture the artist had given Jethro. The cigar-and-decanter piece fit the area perfectly. "I'm impressed."

Jethro pointed to the Kittrell. "Ethan said you helped pick out the picture he gave me."

"He asked for some advice. I warned him we didn't know each other well, but he insisted. The piece reminded me of The Beacon so I thought you'd like it."

"I do, very much."

Did he? His stoic features were so hard to read. "I'm

glad. He wanted to please you. He was very grateful for what you've done for him."

"Good talent deserves to be recognized." He sat back so the waiter could deliver the water and rolls. "Have you ever eaten here?"

"No, but I've wanted to. I've heard lots of good things about The Beacon, even before I came to the Pinnacle." She grinned at him. "I never would have bet I'd be sitting at the owner's table when I finally made it here."

"The world works in mysterious ways."

"So true." She spread butter on one of the warm yeast rolls. "If I hadn't gone to one more dance class, I would never have met Alliyah, never moved to Las Vegas, never have met you."

He eyed her speculatively. "One wonders if there would still be a Jasmine?"

"I don't know. Alliyah's path might have been differ-ent as well. But it didn't happen differently and here we are." She bit into the roll and chewed. And then moaned. "OMG, these rolls are delicious. They practically melt in your mouth. Oh, yum." She pushed the basket toward him. "Keep those over there. Do not let me have another one. Not even if I beg."

"Naturally, I've looked you up," he stated. "But why don't you tell me a bit about yourself?"

He probably hadn't gotten the full report on her yet. She had no doubt whatsoever someone was working on one. "I was a music prodigy as a child. I graduated when I was fifteen, played violin with the Michigan Philharmonic at the age of sixteen while pursuing my PhD at the Univer-sity of Michigan."

"You have a PhD in music and you're a hairdresser?"

"I burned out in music when I was young. I love it, but on my own terms. And I never had that luxury."

The waiter arrived with plates of salmon served with polenta and roasted vegetables. She leaned back to give him access. The food smelled as good as it looked.

"Playing with the Michigan Philharmonic at the age of sixteen is pretty impressive."

"Yes, and I don't regret it. But I wanted to dance and my mom shut me down every time I asked. At eighteen I came into a small inheritance from my father and I took off."

"Where'd you go?"

"New York, of course. It's where dancers go. But it's expensive. And competitive. And I was so new to it. Thankfully, I met Alliyah."

"And ended up in Las Vegas. You fought so hard to dance, why give it up now?"

She shook her head, poked at the fish. Dance would always be a part of her life. Except now it would only be a form of exercise. She still struggled with the change.

"Dancing is considered high-risk employment because contracts can be limited in term and there's the chance of injury. Plus, most of the work is at night. So it's not a good job for a single woman looking to adopt. I have to agree with the last. If I get custody of Jazi, I want to be there for her. As a hairdresser, I can adjust my hours so I can spend part of every day with her."

She laid down her fork and leaned across the table. "Thank you for listening to me last night. Thank you for considering my request."

Eyes on hers, he shook his head, the dim light playing over his dark hair. "Don't get ahead of yourself, Ms. Malone. We don't even know if there's anything to thank me for yet. If I have my wish, there won't be."

Her heart hiccupped at his declaration. Everything she longed for would turn his world upside down. Impulsively she reached across the table and laid her hand on his. "I'll still say thank you because you've given me something I haven't had in a long time. Hope."

* * *

"Good morning." Clay strolled through Jethro's open office door. He carried a manila envelope in one hand.

Jethro nodded for Clay to close the door and then he tossed his pen on his desk and leaned back in his chair. This better be the test results.

His nerves were so frayed he couldn't concentrate. He'd been a beast all morning. His staff mutinied twenty minutes ago and left en masse for an extended coffee break. He'd be lucky if he saw them before lunch. Nothing got in the way of work, but before she left he finally gave in and had his assistant clear his schedule for the day.

"I heard hell froze over up here." Clay dropped into one of the black leather visitor chairs. "I had to come check it out."

"You'll get a front-row seat if those aren't the test results. I'm about to gnaw off my own thumbs."

"These things take time. I had the lab run the tests twice, just to be sure." Clay held out the envelope. "Fresh off the printer."

"And?" Jethro took the envelope, set it in front of him. He'd look at the reports when he was alone.

Clay didn't leave him dangling. "And congratulations, Daddy."

Jethro narrowed his eyes in a glare.

Clay just grinned. "It had to be said. This is a big deal. And if you have your way, it'll never happen again."

"It's for the best."

"Is it?"

A brief knock sounded at the door and then it opened and Jackson Hawke and Ryan Green walked in.

"You don't look dead," Jackson remarked as he settled into the second visitor's chair.

"No, but he's definitely pale. Pasty actually." Ryan perched on the edge of the credenza in front of the window. "He could be dying."

"Ha-ha." Jethro rolled his shoulders. "I'm fine."

"He's not fine."

Jethro glared at the security executive. "I am fine. I just have something to deal with."

He hadn't meant to tell them all, a foolish assumption. They were almost as bad as a pack of women when it came to ferreting out information about each other. And he'd need Ryan's help with the contract and adoption. No need to keep Jackson in the dark when everyone else knew.

Bottom line, he struggled with the secret he already had; no way was he harnessing himself with another one. He fought the urge to pace. The tension in his shoulders was so tight he feared the smallest move might break a bone. His friends looked at him expectantly, their silence a deafening demand. He cleared his throat. Almost wishing Clay would blurt it out saving Jethro from having to say the words.

As if reading his thoughts Clay lifted one brown brow in question.

Jethro shook him off with a minute shake of his head.

"It turns out." Another clearing of his throat. "I have a daughter."

With the words spoken something miraculous happened. Tension drained out of his shoulders and air flowed freely into his lungs. He hadn't even noticed the shallow breaths he'd been taking. Sharing eased some of his pent-up nerves. Not all by any means, but at least he could think again.

"A daughter." Jackson raked a hand through his hair. "No wonder you're freaking." Sympathy shone out of green eyes. He alone knew Jethro's secret.

Still, freaking was a bit strong.

"Does this mean we get to call you Daddy?" Ryan grinned.

Jethro's heart accelerated and tension racketed back into his shoulders. Okay, freaking summed it up nicely.

"I won't be raising her," he announced and filled them

in on the details. "She's better off with someone who loves her," he finished.

"That's a tough decision." All amusement had vanished from Ryan's strong features. "I'm not sure I could walk away."

"You all know how rotten I am at relationships. I wouldn't begin to know how to raise a little girl. I'm doing what's best for her."

"You're not alone, dude," Ryan reminded him. "Four men and a baby. We could make it work."

"Don't forget Grace and Sierra." Jackson tossed his fiancée and assistant into the mix. "They say it takes a village. Well, we are a village."

A lump formed in Jethro's throat. The unhesitating support amazed and humbled him. He shouldn't be surprised, but he was. It made him stop, made him think. But…

"Thank you, my brothers. Seriously, I love you for offering." The words were rusty yet heartfelt. "But it wouldn't be fair to shake up your lives because of an unexpected development in mine. Not when there's an acceptable alternative."

He had nothing of value to offer an innocent child. He was damaged, with no idea how to manage a lasting relationship. Not even his mother had wanted him. She'd tossed him away like yesterday's leftovers.

He'd been found in a Dumpster when he was three weeks old half-starved and suffering from exposure. Lucky to be alive. He sometimes wondered if anyone actually believed that.

Infants usually adopted quickly. But the exposure had damaged his lungs and stomach so he'd been a sickly child. No one wanted to adopt a sick baby.

He'd learned his history when he was six from a foster mother upset because he'd thrown up on her new shoes. He was quickly removed from the home. But how do you get over knowing no one wanted you? Not even your mom. He got moved around a lot after that. His ailments went away, but they said he began acting out, became a problem child.

No. He'd just been trying to prove he was the biggest, the best, the smartest. That he mattered. Even after thirty-five years, he was still trying to prove it.

Talk about dysfunctional. So no, it was best if he were not made responsible for the care and feeding of a toddler. Even if she was the only family he'd ever know. He'd been told, more than once, that he was self-absorbed, but not ever he was that selfish.

Jasmine deserved someone who fought for her, someone who skipped to watch a fake thunderstorm then watched the show with childlike wonder. Someone who spoke to strangers and thought up ways to pamper new mothers.

Of one thing he was certain, life with Lexi would be filled with light, laughter and joy. She'd make every day an adventure of music and dance. Unlike him. His life revolved around work and numbers, boring, steady, reliable numbers, which suited him fine, but hardly rated against the musical arts.

Lexi would cherish Jasmine and that was the best gift Jethro could ever give her.

"Well, if that's decided," Clay glanced at his watch, "I made arrangements for you to see her this morning."

Jackson and Ryan looked at each other and then at Jethro.

"Do you think that's wise?" Jackson asked.

"Probably not." Jethro slid the manila envelope into his top desk drawer and closed it. "But it's something I have to do."

At least once he needed to hold his daughter in his arms.

CHAPTER FIVE

LEXI OPENED THE GATE and walked up the path toward the door of a two-story house. Before she got to the porch, the door opened and a slightly plump blonde waved.

"Hi, Lexi." She stepped aside and a wild-haired child shot out the door and down the shallow step. "She's excited to see you."

"Lexi!" Jazi called out as she raced as fast as her little legs allowed down the walk.

Lexi's heart overflowed with love and she went down on her knees to catch the tiny fireball when she launched herself into Lexi's arms.

"Lexi!" Little arms wrapped around her neck and soft lips smeared something sticky across her cheek.

"Jazi." Lexi returned the smooches, hugging the baby close for a long minute. "I've missed you so much."

"Miss you." Jazi repeated. She framed Lexi's face in her hands and demanded, "Home."

Lexi's heart wrenched. "I know, baby girl. I'm working on it." She turned her attention to Jazi's foster mom, who had to stay within sight of her during the visit. "Hi, Diana, how are you?"

The court had granted Lexi supervised visitation. She'd argued, but in the end, she'd taken what she could get.

"Fine. But it's turning into a busy day. This little one is quite popular today. I know you like to play with her outside, but can you come inside? I want to do a little more straightening up."

At first Jazi's foster mother had been reserved with Lexi,

almost cold. She'd probably been told Lexi had tried to cir-
cumvent the system. But as time went by and she saw Jazi's
affection for Lexi, she'd loosened up.

"Diana, your place always looks great, but sure." Lexi
followed the other woman inside to the family room. "Why
don't you find us a book to read?" she told Jazi as she settled
on the love seat. What did company for Jazi mean? Caseworker visits were usually impromptu, so it wasn't that.
"Who is coming to see Jazi?"

Diana glanced over to where Jazi pawed through the
bookshelf. Keeping her voice low she said, "Her father.
The caseworker called me this morning and said someone
came forward."

"Really?" Adrenaline spiked Lexi's heartbeat. Jethro.
It had to be.

"Yes. They did the tests and he is her father. He asked if
he could see her this morning."

"Fishies." Jazi dropped a book in Lexi's lap.

"Oh, yeah, let's look at the pretty fishies." Lexi opened
the book and mindlessly pointed at the colorful fish. Thankfully Jazi just liked to look at the pictures and flip the pages
so she didn't notice her godmother had suddenly gone brain-
less.

Her hands shook on the stiff pages. *Angels above* she
prayed this was good news and not Jethro deciding to raise
Jazi himself. It was her biggest fear. Because, seriously who
could resist that joyful smile?

"This is exciting, right?" Diana sat down on the matching striped couch. "I know you were seeking custody. But
it's good that she'll be with her father." She mouthed the
last word.

"I hope so."

Diana nodded. "It's always a concern, isn't it, putting a
child in an unknown situation?"

"Yes." Lexi looked down at the book unable to take the
sympathy in the older woman's eyes.

The doorbell rang. For a moment she and Diana locked gazes.

Jazi just took off for the door. She loved company.

"No, Jazi." Diana caught her and brought her back to Lexi.

"Should I go?" Lexi asked.

Diana shrugged. "It's okay with me if you stay. We'll see what they say."

Lexi's heart lodged in her throat. She wanted to believe in Jethro, but the man didn't help build a multibillion-dollar company without having a ruthless streak.

She lifted Jazi into her lap and gave her a squeeze before redirecting her attention to the book. If these were the last minutes Lexi ever had with her goddaughter, she'd make them count. "One little fishy, two little fishy."

"You have reached your destination." Jethro parked his car across the street from a two-story house in a nice middle-class neighborhood. A pretty redhead with a skip in her step opened the gate and started up the walk.

Surprise shook him, along with a healthy dose of desire.

She moved as if she had a constant strain of music running through her head.

Something he understood better now he knew she was a music prodigy.

"The caseworker is meeting us here." Clay reached for his door latch. "That's probably her."

"Hold on." Jethro laid a staying hand on his arm. "That's Lexi Malone. What's she doing here?"

"She has supervised visitation rights."

"Supervised." Jethro watched as the door to the house opened and a blonde woman greeted Lexi. And then a tiny bit of a girl dashed past the woman and flew down the walk to throw herself into Lexi's arms. It was almost painful to watch as the two clung together. "Did you find out the full details of why they've refused Lexi custody? Lexi hinted to me that it has a lot to do with her single status and being able to adequately provide for her, but I get the feeling there might be more to it."

"I'm still working on it." Clay's phone buzzed. "This might be something now." He took the call.

Jethro tuned him out as he watched the scene in the yard until the three disappeared inside. He'd never exchanged a greeting with such intensity in his life. It was an honest, unrehearsed demonstration of love and affection and reinforced his decision. It would be criminal to separate the two.

"I've got the information." Clay tucked his phone away.

"What?"

"The reason they won't allow Lexi custody is partly because of what she told you, that she's a single parent in high-risk employment that requires her to be away from the home at night. But she has a black mark against her because she kept Jasmine without proper authority."

Jethro relaxed. "Red tape. She changed her employment. And I'm sure she was only doing what she thought best in caring for Jasmine after Alliyah's accident," he pointed out.

"That was mentioned, but she has no recent employment history as a cosmetologist so that actually worked against her."

"Tough luck for her." Especially after the heartfelt exchange he just witnessed.

"Her story holds up," Clay stated. "But she could still be playing an angle."

A dark car pulled to the curb and parked, blocking his view of the house. A plump woman in a gray suit that matched her hair climbed from the car.

"That's likely the social worker. So what are you going to do?" Clay repeated. "Are you changing your mind? Are you going to leave Jasmine in foster care?"

"No way." Jethro opened his car door and stepped out. With Clay at his side he crossed the street. "I'd keep her myself before I let her stay in the system."

* * *

Lexi held her breath as Mrs. Leslie walked in followed by Jethro and a large blond man. If they were here then the blood tests must have come back.

Jasmine was his daughter.

"Lexi." Mrs. Leslie greeted her with a smile. "I didn't expect you to be here." Then the smile dimmed as the awkwardness of the moment hit the social worker.

Lexi liked the woman—she reminded Lexi of Mrs. Claus, always cheerful and looking on the bright side of things. Qualities that had to be difficult considering her profession.

"We made arrangements for the visit yesterday." She stood and set Jazi down. "But I should go. Let Mr. Calder have his visit."

The little girl made a stark cry and lifted her arms to be held. Even the toddler felt the tension in the room. Lexi lifted her into her arms. Jazi laid her head on Lexi's shoulder and eyed the men suspiciously.

"Perhaps it would be best if you continued your visit at another time." Mrs. Leslie didn't bother with introductions. "We do have some business to conduct today."

"Of course." Carefully avoiding Jethro's gaze, Lexi stood and tried to hand Jazi off to her foster mother, but the baby shook her head and clung to Lexi. "It's okay, pumpkin. I'll see you another day. Be a good girl and go to Diana."

"No." Jazi was having none of it. "Jab-da, Lexi!" For all it was gibberish the sentiment was clear. She wanted Lexi. When Lexi tried to pull her little arms from around her neck, Jazi began to cry.

Matching tears blurred Lexi's vision. Leaving Jazi like this was breaking her heart.

"I don't mind if Ms. Malone stays." Jethro broke the tension-fraught moment. "If it makes it easier on the child."

Mrs. Leslie visibly relaxed. "Thank you, Mr. Calder. I do

feel it's for the best. Jasmine is still emotionally fragile. I believe Ms. Malone will be a calming influence for your visit."

"I'll be in the kitchen if you need me." Diana made her
escape.

Lexi resumed her seat and rocked Jazi gently. "You're
my big girl, my brave girl. You like Mrs. Leslie. And these
nice men just want to say hello. Come on, pumpkin," she
tickled her ribs, "give me a smile."

The corner of Jazi's mouth twitched up, but she still snuggled close.

"That's my big girl. Everything is going to be all right,"
Lexi whispered, needing the reassurance as much as Jazi.
"I love you."

Mrs. Leslie settled into the corner of the couch and waved
Jethro toward the love seat where Lexi sat with Jasmine.
"Perhaps you'd like to tell me how you know Ms. Malone."

Jethro's gaze circled the room seeking another seat, but
his associate, whom Lexi recognized as Clay Hoffman,
dropped into the corner opposite Mrs. Leslie, which left
a seat squeezed between the two of them or next to Lexi.
He met her stare before sitting. His features were unreadable, leaving Lexi wondering how much he'd reveal to the
caseworker.

When he sat down, the roomy sectional suddenly became
a tight fit. She tried to move over to give him space—and
her some distance—but he just filled in the area she created. From shoulder to knees they were pressed up against
each other.

Yeah, this was comfortable.

"It was Ms. Malone who told me of Jasmine. I wasn't
aware of her existence until Ms. Malone brought her to my
attention."

"Really?" Mrs. Leslie sent Lexi a chiding look. "If you
had information regarding Jasmine, you should have given
the knowledge to Child Protective Services to investigate."

"Yes, well, it was more a hunch than anything else." Lexi noticed he'd made no mention of giving her custody.

"Hmm." Mrs. Leslie didn't sound convinced but she chose not to pursue it. She smiled and suggested, "Shall we get this visit on the way. Lexi, would you like to make the introductions?"

Drawing in a deep breath, she let it out slowly. Rubbing Jazi's back in soothing strokes, she told her softly, "Jazi, this is Mr. Calder. He wants to say hi. Can you say hello?"

Jazi had her head turned away from Jethro and for a moment she didn't move.

"Please." Lexi insisted.

Jazi gave him a quick peak and looked away again.

"See, he's a nice man." Lexi continued to pet her back. To Jethro she mouthed, "Smile!"

He notched a brow at her but nodded.

Okay, what did she reveal? She hadn't planned to be the one explaining this to Jazi. She didn't want to build Jethro up as Daddy to the rescue because—hopefully—he wasn't going to be sticking around. But she really didn't want to advertise their arrangement either.

"Mr. Calder knew your mama." Best to keep it simple.

The toddler sat up and blinked at Lexi. "Mama?"

"Yes." Just as she hoped Jazi snagged on the mention of her mother. "He and Mama were friends. And he wants to meet you. Can you say hi?"

She looked at him from the corner of her dark blue eyes. The glance lasted longer than the last one but she still shook her head.

"Okay, we'll get to know him better first." Lexi swept Jazi up and turned her sideways in her lap so Jazi faced Jethro. "Lexi likes him." Lexi laid her head on his shoulder to show her acceptance.

He smiled. Okay it was a little thin, but he'd made the effort.

"What is your favorite color?" she asked him.

"Blue."

So he was keeping it simple. Probably for the best. "My favorite color is green and Jazi's is—"

"Pink?" he guessed.

"Nope. It's yellow, like her skirt." Lexi tugged at the hem of the white-and-yellow skirt.

"Yellow," Jazi confirmed with a nod.

"What next?" Lexi mused. "When is your birthday?"

Something dark flashed through his eyes, but was quickly gone. He cleared his throat. "May."

No day given, interesting. "Jazi's is in November."

"What else do you want to know, Jazi?"

"Doggy?" Jazi whispered to Lexi.

"Ah, good question. She wants to know if you have a dog."

He shook his head. "No doggy."

Jazi's little brown eyebrows puckered.

"Do you have any animals?" Lexi asked.

She saw the frantic wish to say yes enter his eyes even as he began to shake his head. "No. No pets."

"He has fish." Clay spoke up and nodded to the story-book on the coffee table in front of Lexi and Jazi.

Jethro's eyes lit up. "Yes, I have fish." He picked up the book. "Do you like fish?"

Jazi nodded and pointed at the book. "Fishies!"

"I like colorful fishies." He absently flipped the pages in the book. "I have some that are blue and yellow and orange and red."

"Pretty." Jazi climbed into his lap and began to turn the pages and point at the fish.

Jethro froze. Lexi felt his whole body go still. But he didn't panic. His hold gentle, his voice soft, he hoisted Jazi to a more secure position and began reading the book. Of course she was more interested in flipping the pages to the ones she liked, but he soon adapted and began pointing out fun things on the pages she stopped on.

Across the way Mrs. Leslie nodded and rose to join Diana in the kitchen. Clay followed, giving Jethro some private time with his daughter. Except for Lexi of course. She'd leave too, except Jazi might freak out.

She hid a smile. Jethro just might freak out too.

After a few minutes, Jazi hopped down to get a new book. Lexi took the opportunity to assure him, "She likes you."

He let out a deep breath. "How can you tell?"

"She went to you with no urging. And she's looking for another book for you to read. If she didn't like you, she'd be tugging on my hand demanding I take her outside to play. It's what we usually do when I'm here."

"She's so small. But she's her own little person."

"Yep, that's the way it works." Lexi checked on Jazi's progress. She was still looking through the toy box for the book she wanted, so Lexi asked the question burning in her brain. "Why are you here?"

He focused those unreadable, dark blue eyes on her. "I wanted to meet my daughter."

"So I was right." She lowered her voice. "Please tell me you're going to let me adopt her."

The darkness flashed through his eyes again. Jazi ran up, black curls bouncing, to hand him a Halloween-themed book with five little pumpkins. He helped her climb into his lap. Over her head, he said, "We need to talk."

Lexi paced Jethro's office, from the beautiful wall of glass that overlooked The Strip to the plush seating area and then back again. What did he mean they needed to talk? He knew she wanted to adopt Jasmine. Hopefully he wasn't stringing her along.

But he could. He was her father. He held all the power.

Lexi glanced at her watch, but barely noted the time. Where was he? After they all left Jazi, Lexi received a text from him telling her to meet him at his office.

She was here. Where was he?

His assistant, a pleasant African-American woman in her midforties, let Lexi into his inner sanctum and advised her he'd be along shortly. Twenty minutes made up a lifetime when her future was on the line.

She plopped down in his big black leather desk chair and surveyed his massive desk made of ebony glass. Because she knew it would drive him nuts, she drew hearts around his laptop which sat in the middle of the pristine white page of his leather blotter.

Twenty-three minutes.

Next she rearranged the items on his desk. No pictures, of course. Just a fancy fountain pen—the most *bomb* pen she'd ever used—a letter-opener and a white marble paperweight in the shape of a tiger. No clues to his psyche here.

Why had he been at Diana's? Why had he spent time with Jazi, getting to know her, holding her, when he intended to give her up?

It didn't make sense.

Please, God, she prayed he hadn't changed his mind about wanting a family. Jazi belonged with Lexi. She loved her like her own daughter. Already a void existed in her heart because she missed her so much.

Twenty-six minutes. Time had never moved so slowly.

Seriously!

She dug into her pants pocket for her cell phone. Where are you? she texted him. You can't say we need to talk and then leave me hanging. Send. And then, for good measure, I'm going to start rearranging furniture if you don't get here soon. Send.

Pushing away from the desk she sent the chair swirling round and round. Light and dark flashed before her eyes to an accompanying beat in her head. It started as a tapping of her toes, a roll of her shoulders, and then she popped to her feet unable to deny the urge to dance, to put her frayed emotions into actual motion.

* * *

In the elevator on the way up to his office Jethro stared at his phone. Rearrange his furniture? Crazy woman. What kind of threat was that? An effective one actually. He liked things a certain way. Not at an OCD level, but he didn't care to have people messing with his things.

"What is it?" Clay asked.

"Nothing." Jethro slipped his phone into his pocket. "Lexi is in my office and she's getting impatient."

"Well, we didn't expect to go by Child Protective Services." The elevator stopped and Clay stepped forward. "Do you want me to go back with you this afternoon?"

"Maybe, I plan to take Lexi. If she agrees to my terms. If not, then I'll give you a call."

Clay nodded and exited the elevator. "Good luck with the wild child."

Wild child? Yes, it fit. The elevator went up two more floors and dropped him on the top floor. Hopefully he made it to his office before it sported a new decor.

"What's she doing in there?" he asked when he reached his assistant's desk.

"Waiting," she replied without looking away from her computer screen.

"You haven't checked on her?"

"No. She's not four."

"Are you sure?" he muttered and opened the door. All thoughts of his furnishings fled at the sight that greeted him.

Lexi moved to a tune only she heard. Arms, legs, body, she threw herself completely into the dance. She wore black pants and a short-sleeved tank that clung to her curves. Emotion thrummed through every movement whether she flung her arms wide or ducked into a crouch where she held herself close and then rolled into a full stretch reaching for something just out of grasp.

Her performance reached right into his soul and grabbed hold. He'd already decided to give her Jasmine. But seeing the power of her commitment, the depth of her emotion reflected in her dancing, he was reassured on an elemental level.

With a flick of long legs she knelt and then flowed to her feet and then to her toes, arms outstretched to encompass the world. Finally, slowly Lexi wound down—she rocked back on her heels, her arms coming in so her wrists crossed over her heart, her head dropped forward and she was still.

He detested seeing such despair in someone usually so filled with life. It made him want to wrap his arms around her, offer comfort. He resisted. "It's going to be okay."

She slowly lifted her head. "How can it be if we have to talk? You've changed your mind, haven't you? You want to keep her."

"I haven't changed my mind."

She swung to face him. "Does that mean you'll let me adopt her?"

The urge to touch won out this time. He ran his thumb over the silk of her cheek wiping away a bit of moisture. He hadn't noticed the tears until now, doubted she'd been aware of them at all.

Curling his hand into a fist, he turned his back on her. If this was going to work, he needed to maintain his distance. No more spontaneous acts of comfort.

"That's what we need to discuss."

He glanced around the office, looking for his visitor's chairs. She hadn't so much rearranged his furniture as pushed it all aside. He fetched one of the leather armchairs and set it in front of his desk.

Walking around his desk, he spotted her shoes. With an arched brow, he dropped the red heels on the corner of his desk. Her nervousness apparent, she perched on the edge of her chair, hands clasped in her lap.

"I'm not looking for money or a commitment from you."

Ignoring the pang her comment caused, he retrieved his

chair, which was pushed back against the window, and sat down across from her.

"Yes. You've made that clear."

She leaned back and drew her legs up, rested her chin on her knees. "Now you want to keep her."

"I haven't changed my mind," he repeated absently tracing a heart with his finger. "But I do have conditions."

"What conditions?" Hope lifted her chin, lit up her eyes. She scooted to the edge of her seat. "I'll do anything."

"Good. Then you'll have no problem moving in with me."

CHAPTER SIX

MOVE IN WITH HIM? Hope deflating, Lexi plopped back in her chair. No. She couldn't have heard what she thought she'd heard. "Can you repeat that?"

"I want you and Jasmine to move in with me." Jethro stated.

Nope, it made no more sense hearing it repeated.

"Are you suggesting joint custody?" The very notion made the muscles in the back of her neck twitch. Under no circumstances did she want to be answerable to this man. He was too closed off, too controlling. Life with him would be filled with rules and schedules and accounting for her every movement.

She'd fought too hard for her freedom to surrender it now.

Only for Jasmine would she hear him out.

"No."

Though he appeared intrigued by the option making Lexi sorry she'd suggested it.

"What then? You want us to be roommates?"

"In a sense, and for a limited time. I need to be sure Jasmine will thrive in your care. To that end I must observe you with her, which requires us to be in the same household."

"So to be clear, you'll let me adopt Jazi, but you want to spy on us first."

"Careful, Ms. Malone." Not looking at her, he tapped his pen against his blotter. "Where I recognize my limitations as a parent, Jasmine's well-being is still important to me. I need to know I'm placing her in good hands."

"So you expect me to move in with you?"

"Yes. I believe it's the most expedient way to observe the two of you together."

Add dispassionate to the list of his traits.

Too bad ugly wasn't on the list. Or plain, plain would definitely work. It would make the concept of moving in with a stranger so much easier to contemplate. No, it didn't make sense, but the mind was often irrational, especially when it came to emotions. And living with a plain stranger lurking in the background struck her as much easier to do than fighting a constant attraction for a gorgeous man who wanted nothing to do with her except to observe her interaction with his child.

Luckily, her attention would be focused on Jasmine.

"For how long?" she demanded.

"Three months."

She blinked at him. Three months? "That's forever!"

"No need to overreact. It's a mere blip of time."

"Because you'll be in the comfort of your home, going about your life. I'll be uprooted and spied on."

"A tad dramatic don't you think?"

"Is it?" she pouted.

"You'll be with Jasmine. Isn't that your goal?"

She gritted her teeth. Whatever it took to be with Jazi. "Yes." And then because her feelings were hurt. "Why so long?"

"I need to be one hundred percent sure that you really are the best caregiver for Jasmine. A child is an enormous responsibility and I need to be certain that Jasmine's welfare will be your foremost concern."

Shock rocked through her. "I love Jazi as if she were my very own. I would never let anything jeopardize her welfare!"

"Then you have nothing to worry about."

The grimness of his tone made her stop and think about his words. Oh, goodness. Had his own welfare suffered as a child? Had he been the victim of neglect himself, or worse?

"I'm sorry," she offered softly.

He shrugged. "You don't spend your whole life in foster care without falling victim to a few bad seeds. I don't care to talk about it."

Jethro had grown up in the foster care system. Did that account for his aloofness? The steeliness just beneath the surface?

"Maybe you should," she dared.

His blue eyes iced over. "Do not presume to psychoanalyze me, Ms. Malone."

"No. It's just I've learned that holding things in can be more harmful then helpful." For years her mother dictated how Lexi should spend every minute of her day. Requests for fun events and dance lessons were steadfastly refused. After a while Lexi stopped asking—she held in her discontent to the point she'd come to detest the very thing she'd always loved so much. She dealt with it by leaving and never looking back.

"So how is this going to work? I don't want to lose my apartment or my job. I'm going to need both once the three months are up."

"I'll cover your expenses. Clay talked to Maggie at Modern Goddess. She's agreed to hold your job. I need you to go with me when I travel."

"Seriously? Why?" Sighing, she held up a hand. "I get it. Because you have to be with me to observe me. But couldn't you get one of the hotel nannies to stay with us while you're gone?"

"No."

"But—"

"I won't trust Jasmine's future to anyone else. Go home and pack, Ms. Malone. We pick Jasmine up at four."

A knock came at the door just as Lexi finished cleaning out her refrigerator. Perfect timing. She grabbed the trash on her way to the door.

"Great, you were able to make it early," she greeted a brooding Jethro. She thrust the trash bag into his hands. "Can you toss this down that chute over there? Thanks." She pointed out the garbage chute and then turned back into the apartment, letting the door close behind her.

After a quick glance around to see everything was closed down for the time being, she grabbed her purse and the box of good perishables and headed out. She ran smack-dab into Jethro, who stood arms crossed right on her threshold. He didn't even grunt at the impact that sent her stumbling back into her apartment.

"Careful." His hand shot out gripping her elbow, saving her from dropping the box.

"Sorry." Catching her balance, she slid past him. "I wasn't expecting you to be standing there."

"Surprising."

"What's surprising?" She carried the box to the apartment two doors down and knocked.

"That you wouldn't be expecting me to be standing there when you left me standing outside."

"Is that what you're pouting about? Because I didn't invite you in? I thought it would be quicker if I grabbed the box while you handled the trash so we could get going faster."

"Hello, Lexi," Mrs. Diego yelled when she opened her door. Her smile lacked a few teeth but danced in her fading brown eyes. Gray curls were held back by a pink-and-white-polka-dot headband. "Come on in. Is this your new young man?" In a lower voice that clearly carried to Jethro she said, "He sure is a looker. Makes me wish I were thirty years younger."

Lexi bit back a grin. "Sorry, we can't stay. I'm going to be away for a few weeks, so I brought you my perishables. Can I put them in the kitchen for you?"

"That's so kind of you. Yes, if you wouldn't mind carrying the box." The older woman followed Lexi around the corner to the kitchen. She poked in the box as Lexi put the ice cream in the freezer. "Thank you for thinking of me, dear." Mrs. Diego took her hand and patted it. "You take care now and remember what I told you. Don't be giving away the milk or they won't buy the cow."

"I'll remember." Not that Lexi appreciated the whole cow analogy. Still, she appreciated the concern. She gave Mrs. Diego a hug. "No wild parties while I'm gone."

Lexi made her escape and once again encountered Jethro waiting for her outside the door. The look on his face did not bode well for the car trip.

She planted her hands on her hips. "What?"

"I am not someone you summon like a puppy, Ms. Malone. Certainly not to take out the trash or act as chauffeur."

Puppy? Try Rottweiler.

"I said thank you. And you're the one that wanted to ride together."

"To the social service offices, not all about town."

"Well, per your instructions your men took my car, and I have a few things I need to pick up before we go to get Jazi. So you're stuck taking me to the store." Seeing his scowl grow, she moved past him to the stairs. "I don't see what the big deal is."

"I'm a busy man, Ms. Malone." The bite in his voice came right on her heels. "Every minute of my day is accounted for."

The hairs stood up on the back of her neck as she remembered days, months, years where every moment of her life was accounted for. Some days had been so bad she couldn't breathe she felt so claustrophobic.

"So you got to break away from the office a little early? You're welcome."

His footsteps stopped, then began again. "I enjoy my work."

And she'd loved to dance, missed it more every day. So she got it. "Garage or street?"

"Street."

Exiting the stairwell, she walked through the lobby and outside to the street where a big black SUV sat at the curb. A beeping as he unlocked it confirmed it belonged to Jethro.

He moved with her to the passenger door, but kept his hand on the handle. "What do you need from the store? I'll determine if we need to stop."

Feeling crowded, she rolled her shoulders. Was this how the next three months were going to go? He demanded and she answered?

Oh, heck no.

"Look, I get that you're annoyed at having your precious schedule disrupted. And I understand, and even admire, that you need to know you're giving Jazi over to a safe and nurturing environment, and I'm willing to go through your test to prove I'm worthy. But I'm not a puppet to dance to your tune. If you're willing to treat me like an adult, we can have a discussion about what I need from the store. Otherwise, I'll call a taxi and meet you at social services."

He stared at her with those dark eyes. Her stomach began to clench with each passing second.

"And if I change my mind about the whole deal?"

Her heart plummeted straight to the knot in her stomach. But she jacked up her chin.

"You're not going to do that. Because you recognize that I love Jazi and you want her to have a loving family. Someone who will fight for her. And that's what I'm doing. Being under your thumb for the next few months wouldn't be a true measure of me as a mother. You're supposed to be observing us, not dictating our every move."

His eyes narrowed and his jaw clenched, evidence he didn't care for that statement. Too bad. She waved an agitated hand toward the big SUV.

"You set this scenario up when you sent your men in here

to swoop everything up so quickly. I haven't unpacked Jazi's things because, frankly, it was too painful to look at it all when she was out of my reach. I saw no point in opening the boxes up to take a few things out. So yes, I need to stop by the store to outfit a diaper bag. And because I didn't think of it before they left, we need a car seat too."

Okay that last part was her fault, but hey, he should have a seat for his fleet of cars.

He opened the door and waved her inside. "If you don't treat me like a dog, I won't treat you like a puppet."

"Deal." She got in the vehicle and hoped for the best.

So maybe he'd overreacted slightly. Jethro followed Lexi around the baby department store. She had a point. He was used to giving orders, not receiving them. And it didn't help that she was responsible for turning his whole life upside down. So yeah, her text telling him to pick her up early had hit a nerve.

He trailed her down a lane with car seats displayed from end to end. Who knew there'd be so many models?

Her insistence that he keep his distance didn't help. It was his decision to give Jasmine into her care and he recognized it was for the best. That didn't mean he felt nothing. Every time Lexi pushed him away it was like hearing his mother had thrown him away all over again. The same shock to the head, the same sense of betrayal, the same pain of loss. And the same determination to matter.

That last drove him to branch out beyond Pinnacle Enterprises to be a success in his own right. And it drove him to give Jasmine what he never had, the chance to grow up in a loving environment.

It didn't make watching from the sidelines any easier.

He paused to read some product notes. "How about this one? It exceeds the safety standards."

Lexi came back to examine his choice. She started shaking her head before she reached him. "This is for an infant. We need a toddler size for Jazi."

"It says it converts."

"Hmm. It is a good brand. But let's look at a few farther down the way. We'd be smarter to get one that's for a toddler that converts to the next stage rather than back."

"Good point." Honoring their tentative truce, he refrained from mentioning they were unlikely to reach the next stage in the next three months. He also ignored the pang that accompanied the thought.

He never second-guessed his decisions. Now was not the time to start doing so.

As he moved down the lane, he saw the differences in the sizing Lexi pointed out and made the decision when she waffled between two choices. He propped the big box in her cart and headed for the checkout.

"Wait," she called out, "I want to look at the strollers while we're here. I lent ours to a friend and never got it back." She disappeared around the corner, giving him little choice but to follow. A glance at his watch showed they had time.

He pushed the cart past three empty lanes before finding her. She stood studying a stroller she'd pulled into the aisle. He saw the appeal.

"Sporty." He observed of the three wheeler.

"Yeah, it can be used for walking and jogging as well as everyday use. I like it."

"Then get it."

She sent him a *you're not helping* look. "I'm considering my budget, trying to justify the expense."

Surprised, he checked to see if she was messing with him. He assumed he'd be paying. But no, she sincerely appeared to be struggling with her decision as if she fully expected to make the purchase.

"What the heck." She finally succumbed. "It'll make for more Jazi and me time."

He applauded her reasoning. "Does that mean we're done?"

"Almost. She's grown so much I want to grab a couple of outfits—just enough to last until I can shop more later."

"We've used our extra time, so while you do that I'm going to get in line."

"Good idea. I'll be right there," she promised and rushed away.

He supposed that meant he was in charge of the stroller too. Looking for a box he spotted a tag instead indicating he'd claim the item at merchandise pickup. All the more reason to move on to the checkout counter.

With his destination set, he rounded the corner. And came to a dead stop. The endcap assaulted the eyes with a kaleidoscope of color in the form of stuffed animals. The one that caught his attention was a little blue fish with a large rainbow tail. Jazi's fish book came to mind.

Keep it impersonal, he reminded himself, *maintain your distance.*

Sound advice, the only true way to navigate his way through this situation. And still he found himself reaching for the pretty stuffed fish. Leaving one home for another was always scary. Hopefully, the rainbow fish would give Jazi something to hang on to while the grownups decided her fate.

Lexi quickly grabbed some outfits for Jazi. The little girl would need them. But more than that Lexi needed the time to think. She'd been scrambling ever since she'd agreed to Jethro's condition to move in with him.

It pained her to think of him being hurt in the foster system. He said it didn't matter but she knew better. Still she couldn't let it affect her. They didn't mean anything to each other.

The searing passion she'd experienced in his arms flashed through her head.

She ruthlessly tamped it down.

Cultivating any relationship beyond parent and adoptee would be foolish and only complicate an already convoluted situation.

Which didn't make it any easier to think of living with him.

But she'd do it. Because he held all the power in this situation.

All she had to do was make a good impression on Jethro.

Challenging him less might be a start, but that's not who she was. She'd spent her childhood acquiescing to her mother's wishes, seeking love and approval. All she got for her troubles was discipline and more practice. She mastered the violin and the piano. But whatever she did, her efforts were never enough to meet her mother's exacting requirements. She was always required to do more, better.

At the age of sixteen she got invited to play the winter season with the Michigan Philharmonic. She loved it and hated it. Loved the sense of accomplishment and working with professionals. What she didn't care for was adjusting to the maestro's version of the music. She played the notes fine, but it jarred so strongly with her musical ear that it actually hurt.

Of course her mother accused her of acting out.

Jethro's earlier complaint echoed of her mother's lectures. His controlling demeanor certainly got her back up. She'd known him all of three days and she already recognized domineering as his default mode. But she'd also seen him be supportive, gentle, vulnerable, traits that made him much more approachable, even likable.

Which was way more dangerous to her peace of mind.

Best she focus on his harsher characteristics and stay as far away from him as possible over the next three months. It would be safer for all concerned.

Happier with a plan in place she headed to the front of the store and the checkout stands. Along the way she spotted a stuffed fish, blue with a rainbow tail just like the character in Jazi's book. She tucked it into her arm, the perfect gift to distract her little ball of energy while Lexi and Jethro dealt with red tape.

At the checkout counter, Jethro was waiting for her. The big items had already been rung up and paid for. He smoothly stepped back into line at the empty counter, took the clothes from her and placed them on it. The fish he handed to the cashier. The teenager smiled and put it under the counter.

"Hey!" It all happened so fast Lexi didn't know what to address first. "I said I was buying." Under no circumstances did she want finances to be an issue for him to reject her. She'd made it clear she didn't want money from him and she meant it. "And I want that fish!"

"He already bought the fish." The teenager giggled as she held out the receipt to Jethro. "You two know your kid."

Another customer started piling items onto the counter forcing Lexi to move along. Jethro's hand on her elbow encouraged her toward the door.

Oh, no. She planted her feet. "I said I was going to pay."

"I said I'd cover your expenses for the next three months. That includes Jasmine's as well. I can afford it, Ms. Malone."

She gritted her teeth. "Stop calling me Ms. Malone. And I can afford to care for Jazi."

"Yes, you've made it clear you want nothing from me but my signature. However, those are not my terms. My reasons for giving my daughter up are my own, but dodging monetary support is not one of them."

"I never thought it was." Clearly she'd struck a nerve. Suppressing a sigh, she followed him to the SUV. "That's not the point."

"I know the point." He loaded the stroller into the back. "I suggest we leave this discussion for when we go over the contract."

"Contract?" Her heart leaped. "You never mentioned a contract."

"I didn't think I had to. Of course there will be an adoption agreement. My financial responsibilities will be outlined within it."

Her teeth clicked together again. Her pearly whites were going to be nothing but nubs at the end of three months.

"You're not supposed to have any financial responsibilities," she repeated.

Instead of answering he handed her the fish.

She accepted the plush toy and realized it was an answer of sorts. The care and insight that went into the gift made her stop and think. He'd only spent a few minutes with Jazi, yet he'd noticed she liked stuffed animals and remembered a character from her fish book.

Lexi had been wrong to think his lack of desire for a family came from disinterest or an emotional disconnect. He may wear an aloof facade, but this trip was not the simple connect-the-dots, collect-the-child exercise for him that she thought it was.

Intense emotions festered below his dispassionate expression.

It made her wonder exactly what his reasons were for giving up Jazi.

The thought disappeared when he started to load the box with the car seat into the back.

"Wait." She stopped him. "Let's open that up and put it in the backseat. It'll be easier to do when we don't have Jazi with us."

He glanced at his watch. She bet he was five minutes early to every appointment.

"It'll only take a few minutes. And it will be worth it, I promise. You learn to think ahead when you're dealing with a toddler."

He looked doubtful but he didn't waste time arguing further. He opened the box and handed her the instructions.

She glanced at them. "On the one we had before, you secured the base first."

"There is no base. There's just the chair."

And that's exactly what the instructions showed. Lexi looked up to see he had the seat strapped in place.

"See? Easy. Now we just need to adjust the straps when we load her in."

He cocked a dark brow at her and wordlessly tossed the empty box in the back. "Let's go get our girl."

CHAPTER SEVEN

IT WAS LATE AFTERNOON before Lexi carried a sleeping Jazi into Jethro's penthouse hotel apartment. Her light weight warmed Lexi with a bone-deep satisfaction. This was where she belonged, in Lexi's arms.

She'd held Jazi the day she was born and these last four months without her had been a living nightmare. Lexi vowed never to lose her again.

The foyer led to a large living room furnished with sleek, modern pieces. Lexi stepped into the room and saw floor-to-ceiling windows made up the exterior wall. On the far end of the area a dining room held a table big enough to seat eight. Bar stools lined up against a kitchen island though the kitchen was out of sight.

An in-wall aquarium behind the bar in the living room held the fish he'd told Jazi about.

"This way," Jethro said. "We'll get her settled then I'll give you a tour."

He'd offered to carry Jazi, but she was too precious for Lexi to give her up just yet.

He led the way down a hall and opened a door on the right. "This will be you." Moving on a few feet, he opened a door on the left. "And this is Jasmine." He scowled at the low, short child's bed. "There's been a mistake. This should be a crib. I'll call down and get housekeeping to send some-one up to fix it."

"No." Lexi placed Jazi on the bed and covered her with a blanket conveniently draped over the foot of the bed. "I told them to set up the bed. Diana recently told me Jazi has taken to climbing out of her crib. At least this way if she gets up in the night, she won't have a four-foot drop."

Jethro ran a hand over the back of his neck. "No, we wouldn't want that."

Lexi fussed over Jazi for another couple of minutes, taking off her shoes and tucking Rainbow, her new pet fish, under the blanket with her.

She looked up at Jethro. "Thank you for this," she said. "Thank you so much for giving her back to me."

He went still before slowly nodding. "We need to make it through the next three months first."

"I haven't forgotten." Undeterred she kissed Jazi's soft cheek. "But that's just a matter of time. Soon it'll be the two of us and we can start our life together." She exited the room and pulled the door mostly closed, leaving only an inch open so she could hear Jazi if she woke up.

When she glanced up at Jethro, his eyes were shuttered. He nodded toward double doors at the end of the hall. "That's me."

"Oh. You're close."

He made no comment to that. Didn't really need to. Still, she found it a little unnerving to know he was only a few feet down the hall.

From the desk in her room and the shelves and books, she figured the space must have been his office. "I'm putting you out."

"It's only for a few months." He shrugged her statement away. "I do most my work downstairs. It's no big deal."

He struck her as a creature of habit, so she rather thought it was more of a deal than he made out, but this arrangement was his idea so she was all right with that. She'd do her best to keep Jazi's sticky little fingers out the books but if he suffered a few casualties, it was on him.

He showed her the bathrooms, she and Jazi each had their own, the kitchen—a cook's dream—and the media room. Like the living room, the furnishings were sleek and modern throughout but built for comfort. It was all a tad too minimalist for her tastes but it fit the game the themed hotel was based on so she got it. And the sheer luxury of it made up for a deficit of style.

The apartment exceeded the size of hers by double the square footage yet still seemed small with Jethro standing next to her. The idea of sharing this space with him for the next three months unnerved her on so many levels.

In the kitchen she opened the refrigerator and a couple of cupboards. They were empty except for ground coffee beans and stale crackers.

"I eat out a lot or order my meals from room service." He explained. "I don't expect you to cook, but I understand you'll need to have food on hand. Make up a list and I'll have groceries delivered."

"That's okay. I prefer to do my own shopping." Yep, she was already looking for an excuse to escape for a few hours. "I like to cook."

He lifted a dark brow at her claim, but didn't challenge her. "Tomorrow I'll introduce you to Velveth. She's in charge of the hotel nanny service. We do an extensive background check on the nanny candidates, and they are all trained in CPR and self-defense."

Outrage and hurt lifted her chin. "Are you saying I can't take Jazi out on my own?"

"No." His immediate response took the edge off her rising ire. "But if you need to go out without Jasmine, I want you to use the service."

Shaking off the tension, she nodded. "Okay. That would work when I go to the gym. Is it okay to use the hotel facilities for my workout? Then I'd still be on-site if Jazi needed me."

"Actually—" He stopped and then continued on. "That's a good idea. The gym is on the fourth floor."

"Great." She wondered what had tripped him up but let

it go. They were actually communicating without arguing. All was well.

"I have work. I'll leave you to get settled."

"Okay." Her spirits rose. She'd breathe easier once he left.

"I'll have my assistant make a reservation for dinner. I'll collect you and Jazi at six."

"Sounds like a plan." She followed him to the door, held it open all the while resisting the urge to shove him through it and snap the lock. "See you later, dear."

Little brat. Jethro brooded on Lexi's farewell message all the way to his desk. Too strange having people share his space.

Except for a few rare occasions when he had to host one of his foster brothers, it had been years since he'd had anyone stay over with him. He liked to keep his private space private. One of the contributing factors in why his long-term relationships failed. Long term being nine months and that experience only lasted so long because she'd been in the middle of a merger and too busy to notice the distance he maintained between them.

He foresaw Lexi and Jazi leaving an indelible stamp on his life.

He opened his bottom drawer and pulled out the contract Ryan had sent down. Lexi kept insisting she didn't need financial compensation, but today he'd seen the prices of baby equipment and how much stuff came with a child. And there was Jazi's future to consider—he wanted her to be able to go to a decent college. He needed to do his part. Locating that section, he made a few significant changes.

After booting up his laptop, he sent Ryan a short email outlining the changes. Five minutes later the man stood in his office.

"I thought this woman didn't want any money from you." Ryan dropped into a visitor's chair.

"You know it's not about the money for me. I'm not attempting to dodge my financial responsibilities."

"Obviously not." Ryan held up his phone, where he'd apparently read the email. "What changed your mind? Did Ms. Malone change her tune?"

"Quite the opposite." He told Ryan how appalled Lexi had been when he paid for the few items at the baby store. "I understand the strategy behind keeping money out of the equation when she approached me. But once I recognized Jasmine as mine, the situation changed. I'm not a stingy man."

"Of course not."

"Doesn't she realize by refusing my assistance she's insulting me and doing an injustice to Jasmine?"

"It's not about the support," Ryan stated. "It's about control."

"What's that mean? I've seen her finances—I know she can afford to support Jasmine. But with my help, they'd both have a better quality of life."

"And that monthly payment would be a permanent link to you."

"Why is that a bad thing?"

"Consider if the circumstances were reversed."

Jethro scowled. "I don't see the problem."

"Because you're being stubborn. If you adopted a child and were trying to raise her would you want a monthly reminder going to the child's mother? Wouldn't it make you worry that someday she might decide she wants to be a part of the child's life?"

"That's not going to happen."

"Are you sure? You seem pretty involved."

"Of course I'm involved. They're in my home. But it's temporary." He tossed his pen down on his desk. "When the three months are up, I'll be out of the picture."

"Except for a monthly payment."

"Put it in a trust if that makes you happy."

"It does actually." Ryan nodded his approval. "With a bank as trustee it takes you out of it."

"Glad you're happy. Just know this, the more Lexi protests, the more I intend to add."

Suspicion filled Ryan's eyes. "Maybe that's her game."

The corner of Jethro's mouth quirked up. "No. She's a dancer not an actress. She's made it clear she doesn't want anything from me, but I didn't sign up to be a sperm donor. I intend to make sure my daughter never wants for anything. Ms. Malone will just have to deal with it."

Already imagining Lexi's arguments, he handed the amended document across the desk to Ryan. She'd just have to get over it.

Providing financial stability was the least he could do for his daughter.

Lexi found that both her and Jazi's things were already unpacked. Wow, she could get used to this hotel life. Except it left her nothing to do.

So, of course, she snooped.

She started in her room. Designed in muted greens and beige, the furnishings had the quality and comfort she'd expect in a luxury hotel. No sense wasting time there, she headed straight for the books in the shelves. And discovered Jethro either bought the books for appearances or had a broad taste in literature. The financial books and periodicals were obviously his. There were also mysteries, biographies, nonfiction history books and some poetry.

The poetry had to be for show. Or maybe a gift from some hopeful woman? Lexi just couldn't picture Jethro reading poetry.

Now this book, yes. She pulled out *The Art of War*, by Sun Tzu, and thumbed through the pages. Did he use it for game play or the boardroom? Probably both. A quote popped out at her.

It talked about subduing the enemy without fighting, about evading the enemy if she lacked strength.

Yeah, she could get behind that.

Yep, evade and avoid, that was her plan. Except seeing it put like this made her feel itchy. She didn't care for the concept of being too weak to engage. She dropped the book on her bedside table. Maybe she'd glean a few tips on how to handle the book's owner.

Next she checked on Jazi. No surprise she'd kicked off the blanket Lexi had draped over her. The child hated to be restricted and always had. It was a struggle to keep her properly covered. Blankets, shoes, socks and jacket constantly got tossed aside. Pants and shirts, too, if she had her way.

Except for the child, there was nothing of Jethro's in the room. Totally pink, the staff had taken the time to unpack all the wall art, blankets, lamps, rugs and put the full nursery together. A nice gesture for a temporary situation. Jazi should feel right at home. In this room if none of the others. She'd adapt as she'd already had to do so many times in her short life.

Lexi looked forward to the time when it was just the two of them and they could build a stable life together.

She wandered down the hall to Jethro's room. Maybe she should look for a house during these three months, consider putting down real roots. She hesitated with her hand on the knob knowing he'd see her snooping as a violation of his privacy.

Knowledge was power. Even the few verses she'd read of battles and war had shown her that. Just a peek, she promised herself.

Wow. Where her room was understated luxury, this room shouted penthouse. From the custom king-size bed, to the sunken conversation area with the fireplace, to the glass-and-crystal bar complete with mini fridge and wine cooler, the room offered decadent comfort. The earthy greens and browns grounded the space and offset the futuristic elements to the art and accessories.

Impressive—oh, yeah—but if she hoped to find insight into Jethro she was doomed to disappointment. The art was interesting but similar to pieces in her room. Which meant it came with the room.

He knew his wines; she'd give him that. Okay, that was something. Reading a few more labels she'd even say he was a bit of a connoisseur.

The mini fridge held cola, some nice cheeses, stuffed olives and dark chocolate ice cream. Humming her approval, she closed the door and rounded the corner into the closet. Female to her core, she just slipped down the wall and sat staring. Envy curled her toes.

A new life goal bloomed inside her. Someday she wanted a closet like this.

Forget the bedroom, she'd just move in here. It was nearly as big as her room and included a lounge for her to sleep on. And a chair if she desired company. Racks, shelves, hooks and nooks ringed the room as well as a three-way mirror. In the middle a marble-topped island with a small sink housed drawers.

The beautiful space was wasted on Jethro's black suits and white shirts. Oh, the color she could bring to this room. Shoes there, purses in those slots. Her jackets on that wall, dance gear in the drawers—

Stop. Focus.

At first she didn't think there was any evidence of Jethro in here either.

But she couldn't be more wrong. The order, neatness and overall preciseness of everything broadcast Jethro's need for dominance and control. She pushed to her feet and prowled down the line of black suits and white shirts. Seriously, someone needed to tell him gray was the new black when it came to power suits.

Then again, maybe it was his way of staying in the background. If so, he was deluding himself. His sheer presence radiated power. So she supposed it didn't matter what he wore.

A picture frame caught her eye. On the marble counter

close to the far end were two frames standing back to back so a picture could be seen from either side of the island. A ratty crocheted cap rested between the two photos. The first shot was of a younger Jethro, in his late teens, and a petite woman with short blond hair and some well-earned wrinkles around her eyes and mouth. She had her hand on his shoulder and he wore a huge grin and the crochet cap. In the other picture the Fabulous Four surrounded the dainty woman.

The woman must be Harman, the foster mother who brought the four boys together and made them a family, one of Jethro's foster brother's had told her, Lexi would bet money the woman crocheted the cap. It said a lot that Jethro had kept it all these years and that he kept her picture not just where only he would see it, but where he would see it daily.

It revealed a capacity to care deeply, something his dispassionate facade belied.

She felt him before she saw him. Jethro. With no thought at all she dropped to her hands and knees. As if she could hide.

"Ms. Malone." Shiny black loafers appeared in her view.

"I lost an earring." She felt her ear, removing the gold hoop. She held it out. "Look at that it rolled all the way in here." Popping to her feet she smiled innocently.

He lifted one dark brow. Nope, not buying it.

His strong features were marble hard, his stance set, quite intimidating. She half expected to see steam coming out of his ears. But his eyes were remarkably calm.

He knew he'd caught her snooping, probably came back early for that very purpose.

She hated to be predictable.

"Okay, you caught me. I was snooping through your rooms. But it's your fault."

He crossed his arms over his chest. "Why? Because I brought you here?"

"Yes."

"And I thought it was a given we'd respect each other's privacy. Perhaps we need to discuss the rules of common courtesy."

Heat flooded into her cheeks. "That won't be necessary, no."

"Then explain to me why you're in my closet."

"I was just trying to get to know you. We're going to be living together for three months yet I know so little about you. I was hoping a peek at your private space would give me some insight."

"And what did you deduce?"

"Not much. You have a wide interest in reading, good taste in wine, and this closet is a physical manifestation of your need for control and order. So you needn't worry, your secrets are safe." She stormed past him into the bedroom. "I don't get it. You're a patron of the arts, but you don't even have anything personal on the walls."

"When you have all your possessions stripped from you, you learn not to invest yourself in them."

What a heartbreaking revelation. One he regretted as soon as he said it. She saw it in his eyes and the stiffness in his shoulders. Even she'd had things, in fact, after her dad died, things took the place of affection in her household.

"That had to be a long time ago."

"Some lessons are hard to unlearn."

"I know you grew up in foster care. I'm sorry. It must have been a difficult childhood." She kept her tone matter-of-fact because—

"I don't need your pity, Ms. Malone."

Because of that.

"And you don't have it, Mr. Calder." Leaving the intimacy of the bedroom, she led the way to the living room, checking on a sleeping Jazi, as she walked by. "I feel for the child you were. You aren't that child anymore. You're a powerful man, Jethro. Nobody's going to take anything from you that you don't willingly give up."

"Indeed. I'm glad we understand each other. There will be no repeat visits to my closet."

"No."

"Good."

"So why are you here?" She planted her hands on her hips. "Checking up on me already?"

He mimicked her. "You mean to see if you were messing in things you shouldn't?"

Okay, her insecurities were showing. She so walked into that one, especially when she suspected he'd known she was snooping.

"You didn't answer your phone," he said.

"Oh." She looked around for her purse, which held her phone. She collected it from where she'd dropped it in an armchair. Neither of them sat. "I didn't hear it. What did you need?"

"I've made two appointments for you tomorrow morning. One with the nursery services and one with security."

Definitely hoping to catch her snooping. The message so could have waited.

"I was concerned when you didn't answer. This is a new place to you and Jasmine. Something could have happened."

"Oh." That took the defiance from her sails. The sincerity in his voice too real to be a ploy. "Thanks for checking on us."

"How's Jasmine settling?"

"Fine. She's been asleep, which is a good sign. She tends to have an internal radar that wakes her when things are uneasy."

"Good. I'll get back to work." He turned into the foyer. "Stay out of my room."

She rolled her eyes.

"I saw that."

"Liar."

He glanced at her over his shoulder as he opened the door. "I never lie, Ms. Malone. I don't have to."

Shortly after Jethro made his exit, a sound drew her from her contemplations. Jazi.

Lexi jumped up and rushed to her girl. Sleepy-eyed and clutching Rainbow she stood in the middle of her room. When she spotted Lexi, her little face lit up with a big smile and she reached out her arms to be held.

Heart squeezed tight, Lexi lifted the toddler into her arms. Sweet, sweet moment. "Hello, sleepy girl."

"Lexi! Hi!" Little arms ringed her neck and a tiny bow mouth bussed her cheek. "Love you."

"I love you, too, pumpkin. Uh-oh, you're a wet little girl. Let's get you changed." Lexi made quick work of changing Jazi, listening to her chatter all the while. Lexi only understood the odd word here and there. Didn't matter, she drank in every syllable. Too soon to get Jazi ready for dinner so Lexi put clean pants on her and set her on her feet. "Do you like your new room?"

"Yes."

"Shall we check it out? Find where everything is?"

"Yes." Jazi ran to the bookshelf and began pulling out books.

"Whoa, pumpkin." Lexi smiled at the toddler's enthusiasm. "Let's do this one at a time."

For the next hour, she patiently helped Jazi explore her new environment and unpack the bag Diana sent with the girl. To Jazi's joy she found the fish book tucked into the bag. Of course they needed to read the book right now. Jazi hunted up Rainbow and climbed into Lexi's lap.

After a while it was time to put the book aside and get ready for dinner. For Jazi that meant a yellow dress with black piping. For Lexi it was a royal blue sheath dress.

To keep her occupied until Jethro arrived, Lexi carried Jazi to the media room. Snuggled into a plush recliner with the girl curled on her lap, Lexi giggled to the outrageous antics of a sponge and his starfish friend when Jethro strolled into the room.

Jazi popped up and clapped her hands. "Daddy."

CHAPTER EIGHT

DADDY. THE WORD ROARED through him like fire destroying all resolve in its path. Everything in him longed to claim this child as his. Daughter. Family. Continuity. All he'd ever wanted sat within his reach, cuddled in the arms of the woman who drew him in ways he'd never imagined.

Terror replaced the want. Except for Mama Harman, he'd managed to sabotage every relationship he'd begun, and that one lasted only because she'd refused to give up on him. He didn't know how to let them in, to share. In order to survive, he'd built up walls he found impossible to let down.

Emotionally deficient, Kimberly had called him. And he couldn't refute it.

Though the Lord knew he'd shared more with this impossible woman Lexi than anyone else.

As emotions warred within him, Lexi's raced over her expressive features. Shock, horror, sympathy came and went as she corrected the child. "No, no pumpkin. Remember, this is Mr. Calder. He's the nice man who is helping us."

Clearly Jasmine had not learned the word from her.

"Man," Jazi said.

"Jethro," he stated, his voice huskier than usual as resolve settled in him. He'd given his word and he'd keep it. There was no denying the love between these two. He wouldn't take that from his daughter. "Mr. Calder is a bit of a mouthful."

"Jethro." Jazi mimicked and smiled.

His heart cracked. He cleared his throat. "We should go or we'll be late for our reservations."

"Jethro." Lexi made a step toward him.

He shook his head and stepped back, refusing her pity. "I'll meet you at the door."

Jethro took them to The Beacon where they sat at the chef's table in the kitchen. It was quite the show, loud and chaotic, a dance of creativity and control and heavenly scents.

The noise made up for Jethro's silence. He was quiet during dinner and who could blame him? Lexi knew this was proving more difficult for him than he'd expected. Something flashed in his dark blue eyes and she feared the additional exposure to Jazi had him questioning his decision.

Dang it. He'd brought this on himself by demanding they live with him.

She prayed he didn't change his mind. This was only the first day and Jazi was so sweet, so beautiful, so clever, she made it impossible not to love her. How would he feel three months from now?

Lexi could only trust he'd keep his word. Otherwise she'd drive herself nuts over the next ninety days.

She kept up a constant chatter through the awkward meal, entertaining Jazi and including Jethro, though he added little to the conversation. Lexi wanted to apologize for Jazi's blunder.

She totally should have anticipated something like that would happen. As far as the rest of the world was concerned, Jethro would be raising the child. Someone may well have called him Jazi's father. But there was no way to address the topic in front of the child, so it would wait.

The chef came over to make sure they were enjoying their meal. Jethro unbent long enough to compliment his steak and lobster. And she praised her lamb in cabernet sauce as the best meal she'd ever eaten, a truth belied only by the tenseness at the table that made it hard to concentrate on food. He frowned at the uneaten food on her plate but seemed appeased when she asked to take the leftovers with her.

Back in the penthouse, she took Jazi off for a bath and to get her ready for bed. Jazi loved the water and played gleefully in the tub. Lexi enjoyed the time and allowed the toddler her fun until her knees protested.

"Time to get out," she told Jazi.

"No." The little girl shook her head and dunked her yellow rubber ducky.

"Yep. Stand up now and let me lift you out."

"No." Jazi continued to play.

"Okay. One more minute." Being smarter than a twenty-three-month-old Lexi found the plug and pulled it. Water and bubbles disappeared down the drain and Lexi lifted Jazi out of the tub and wrapped her in a soft towel. Jazi pointed to the ducky and Lexi reached into the tub to grab it.

Jazi took the opportunity to run off giggling as she went.

"Oh, no, you don't." Lexi made a grab for her but caught only towel. And then there was a naked little girl on the loose.

Lexi pushed to her feet and dashed after her. She entered the bedroom in time to see Jazi running out the door. Lexi gave chase, thrilling Jazi. Her shrieks of glee echoed down the halls.

"Got you." Lexi swept her up and swaddled her in the towel. "Wicked child." She tickled her causing her to laugh and scream.

The door at the end of the hall opened and Jethro stood there. "Everything okay?"

"Bath time escapee." Lexi advised. "I have it under control. Say good night Jethro."

"Night, Jethro."

"Good night."

She felt the weight of his regard until she cleared the bedroom door. She sighed her relief but it was short-lived as he came to lean against the doorjamb and watched as she diapered Jazi and dressed her in warm pajamas.

Tucking her into bed, Lexi kissed Jazi's petal-soft cheek. "Night-night, pumpkin."

"No. Book."

"You want a story."

"Yes."

"Okay." Pretending Jethro wasn't observing her every move, Lexi held up a finger. "But only one."

Jazi held up her hand with all the fingers spread wide.

"Five?" Lexi laughed and closed her hand around the tiny digits. "You don't even know how much that is. Two, final offer. Go pick out your books."

She came back with her fish book and then ran to the couch where she'd left Rainbow. With the stuffed fish tucked under her arm she crawled into Lexi's lap. Lexi kissed the black curls and opened the book. A glance at the door found it empty.

Since this was the little girl's first night in a new place, Lexi stayed with Jazi until she fell asleep. A task that took longer than she anticipated due to the toddler's long afternoon nap. Lexi left a lamp on low and pulled the door half-closed. She wanted to be able to hear if Jazi stirred in the night.

She went in search of Jethro to make her apology, but didn't find him in the common rooms. Standing outside his bedroom door she heard music, a slow bluesy jazz and decided not to disturb his peace.

She thought about going to bed because early to bed would be early to rise for her little charge, but Lexi was a night owl. As a dancer in a casino production, her schedule had practically been the reverse of norm. She'd left dancing behind, but old habits were hard to break. Not to mention she was a bit antsy in this new place herself.

After changing into more comfortable clothes, she strolled down to the kitchen and made a pot of coffee. Then she sat at the table and started a list for groceries. From there she made out a menu for the week, adding a few items to her shopping list as she went.

She drummed her fingers on the table. And what about laundry? According to Jethro the hotel handled that as well. Uh-uh. No way was she letting strangers wash her undies. Not to mention a two-year-old went through a lot of clothes in a week. There was a concierge for the penthouse floor; maybe there was a laundry as well. Grabbing her key, she went in search of what she could find.

The floor held two penthouse suites that spanned half the hotel, one on the north, one on the south so they both had views of the strip. The elevators were in the middle. Lexi padded barefoot down the hall until she found an unmarked door. It opened at her touch.

And yes, there was the trash chute and next to it a laundry chute, a good indication there was a laundry on the floor. She kept going trying doors along the way.

"Bingo." At door number three she hit pay dirt. The small room held two industrial-sized washers and dryers, and one set of standard-sized. "Perfect."

"May I help you, Ms. Malone?"

"Oh." Lexi jumped at the cool male voice. She swung around. A slim, dark-haired man stood just inside the door, hands clasped behind his back. "Hello. You know my name."

"Of course. I'm Brennan, executive concierge. Mr. Calder instructed me to assist you as needed, however, I was expecting a phone call not a visit."

"Oh, well, I was looking for the laundry. Do you suppose it will be okay for me to use these machines?"

"That would be highly unusual, Ms. Malone. Most inappropriate." Brennan moved to stand between her and the machines as if to protect them from her. "There are bags provided in the suites. Just place your items in the bags and I shall see they are properly cleaned."

"See, that's the thing. I don't know you well enough to

let you handle my underthings." Lexi smiled to show no hard feelings. "I'm sure you understand."

Pink flushed bright against his pale complexion. "I can assure you there is no impropriety, Ms. Malone."

"I'm sure. I'd still prefer to do my own laundry."

Relief flooded his features as he looked beyond her. "Ah, Mr. Calder."

"Brennan."

Lexi swiveled toward the door. "Jethro."

He stood in the doorway, hands on hips. Except for the jacket, he still wore his suit except the buttons of his white shirt were undone at the neck and the sleeves were rolled up exposing his hair-dusted forearms.

"Thank you for coming." Brennan rushed forward. "If I might explain—"

Jethro held up a hand. "I heard. I think it's best if we allow Ms. Malone to handle her own laundry."

Brennan nearly sputtered in his indignation, but he pulled himself together and nodded. "Very well, sir. Ms. Malone, I'll provide you with a list of times the machines are available." With a nod he departed.

Jethro met her gaze, gestured for her to precede him. He was annoyed.

With good reason. There'd been no need for Brennan to drag Jethro into this. Lucky he had, though, since she hadn't been making much headway.

"I'm sorry you were drawn into this, but I'm used to doing for myself and with the machines right here it seems ridiculous to have someone else taking time to do what I'm perfectly willing to do." Somehow it felt too intimate to bring up her underwear with him.

He said nothing. They reached the penthouse and she used her key to let them in.

"Good night, Ms. Malone."

"Wait." Maybe his reticence wasn't about the laundry at

all. "I was looking for you earlier." She waved toward the living room. "Can we talk for a minute?"

He gave a shake of his head. "I'm in the middle of reading a report."

"Please, it'll only take a moment."

His jaw clenched, but he followed her into the living room.

"Would you like some coffee?" she asked, nervous now she had his attention. "I made a pot earlier, but it's still hot."

"Sure. I take it black."

She half expected him to follow her into the kitchen to prompt the discussion he obviously wanted no part of but he didn't. She poured two mugs, doctored hers with cream and sugar and carried them to the living room.

He hadn't bothered to turn on the lights. He stood silhouetted against the window, the flickering glow of the strip. From this distance she had no view of the hotels, just the brilliance of the lights that rivaled the sunset in color and brightness. And his bold, strong form.

Hands in his pockets, shoulders straight and stiff, he looked so alone it broke her heart.

She set the mugs on the tray on the ottoman and went to him.

"I want to apologize for what happened earlier with Jazi," she said gently. "I know it was a shock and not what you wanted."

"It wasn't your fault. You were surprised as well." He spoke to the window.

"I was." Relief that he didn't blame her steadied the hand she placed on his shoulder. "But I should have foreseen someone would put thoughts of daddy in her head. I'm sorry."

"You're worried this changes things."

She remembered the vulnerability in his eyes and held her breath. "Does it?"

"No."

Oh, she wished she could believe that. "It would be easier for you to make a clean break."

That brought him around. There was no softness in his features now. "My mind won't rest easy until the three months are up."

Her gut compressed. "I'll take good care of her," she promised.

"I know. And still her safety is too important to take chances on."

She nodded. It was the one argument she couldn't fault. For now, she'd put her faith in him.

"Do you mind if I go down to the gym for a while? Jazi is out and I'm too antsy to sleep yet."

He glanced away but not before she saw a spark of panic quickly subdued. He shrugged. "Don't be too long."

"I won't." She bit back a small smile at the show of nerves at being alone with Jazi. "And I'll keep my cell with me. Call me if she wakes up and I'll be right here."

"I think I can handle a sleeping child."

"Hmm." Lexi hoped so. Hoped Jazi didn't wake with one of her screaming fits. The yoga pants and tee she wore were fine for a short workout, so she grabbed her key and headed for the door. "Thanks. And thanks for helping with the laundry. I'll feel much better doing it myself."

"Don't thank me. I did it for purely selfish reasons."

Her brows jumped in surprise. "Really? And what reasons are those?"

"I don't like the idea of any other man touching your underwear."

Jethro wondered when he'd become such a masochist as he watched the awareness pop into Lexi's pretty eyes. The soft blue irises lit up like the sea on a sunny day. Or maybe it was wishful thinking and the reflection of the lights from the strip behind him.

She stood frozen for a moment. And then her gaze raked him from head to toe and back and when those stunning eyes met his, the heat in them had nothing to do with the sun and everything to do with wanting.

His body urged him forward, but his mind blocked the move so he jerked in place.

Desire tightening her features, she stepped back and shook her finger at him. "No fair muddying the waters. I'll be back in an hour."

She practically ran to the door.

Jethro cocked his head unable to resist watching her exit, enjoying the view of her swaying hips in snug yoga pants and the soft bounce of her breasts from the side once she got through the door.

He turned back to the window and the view outside, seeking a diversion from thoughts of long dancer legs entangled with his as he feasted on lush, cherry-red lips.

She tempted him beyond reason.

Because if he were being reasonable, he'd admit she was right and make a clean break from her, from the daughter he was determined to do right by.

The Lord knew he'd gotten nothing done today while brooding about doing just that. He'd used the excuse of being concerned for Jazi's welfare, and he was, but he no more believed Lexi would purposely do anything to harm the child than he would. At dinner she'd burnt her own fingers moving a hot dish out of Jazi's reach rather than risk the girl touching it.

But he wasn't giving them up.

Not one day before the three months was over.

These were the only days he'd have with his daughter, with the bright and beautiful woman she'd call mother. They might be from the point of view of observer, but he'd still have memories to look back on and cherish.

Except for anything work related, he always felt like an outsider, and neither Lexi nor Jazi was expecting anything from him so this should be a simple stroll down the boulevard.

As long as there were no more tantalizing moments like the one they'd just shared. He'd have to control his tongue. And other body parts.

Who'd think laundry would be the thing to trip him up? He'd been annoyed when he got the call from Brennan that Lexi was snooping through the utility hall. What could she possibly want back there? When he heard her mention strange men in the same sentence as her underthings, his agitation spiked from annoyed to red-hot fury. By the time he reached the laundry room door, she'd had his full support.

Brennan better heed Jethro's orders. He'd fire any man who put his hands on any item of Lexi's clothing more intimate than a winter jacket.

"Fool," he muttered. "Pull it together. Time to get back to work."

He spied the coffee Lexi had poured for him and took it with him to his room where he gathered up his tablet. He carried both back down to Jazi's room where he settled in the armchair. Babysitting was new to him. Best he stayed close in case he was needed.

She slept on her side with one little hand under her cheek and the other flung out at her side. She'd tossed her covers aside, but Lexi had dressed her in fleece pajamas with feet, and the room was fairly warm, so he chose not to disturb her and risk waking her.

He reached for his tablet quite sure they'd both make it through this experience better if she remained asleep.

Forty minutes later she sat straight up in bed and looked at him.

He froze, hoping she'd lie down and go back to sleep. What would he do if she didn't? No tears, he prayed. He should have asked Lexi for more instructions before he let her go.

"Jethro." Jazi blinked a couple of times. Then she slid from the bed. She got the fish book from where Lexi had left it on the bedside table and brought it over to him. Holding the book she lifted both arms up, demanding to be picked up.

He set his tablet aside and lifted her into his lap.

"Story." She snuggled around until she got comfortable and opened the book.

Turned out he didn't have to do anything but follow her lead. "Okay, but only for a few minutes and then it's back to bed."

"No bed." She shook her head. She pointed to the blue fish. "Bow."

"Yes, that fish looks like Rainbow." He'd never held anything so precious in his life. She was soft and warm and weighed no more than a feather. He breathed in the sweet scent of baby powder and decided to let Lexi deal with putting her back to sleep when she returned. He feared he'd have a hard time denying her anything. Better delay than defeat. "Shall we name all the colors in her tail? There's blue and green and yellow."

Lexi heard giggles as soon as she walked in the door from the gym. She peeked in the bedroom door and found Jazi curled up in Jethro's lap. He was reading her book in character. His masterful falsetto was what had Jazi laughing. It made Lexi's lips twitch too.

When a laugh escaped, he glanced up, saw her. He lit up with relief. Making no bones about it, he stood up plopped the toddler in her arms, kissed Jazi on the top of her head, kissed Lexi hard on the mouth and escaped out the door.

His taste on her lips, she watched him go.

What a way to end her first day.

The next morning Lexi awoke to find Jazi in bed with her. Moving slowly, Lexi managed to slip out of bed without disturbing the sleeping child. Diana had told Lexi that Jazi had a habit of wandering around at night.

After tucking the covers around her, Lexi slid into the bathroom for a quick shower.

It had taken forever to get the toddler to sleep last night. Best she stay down as long as possible this morning.

Lexi pulled on jeans and a purple sweater that fell to her thighs. Jazi woke up as she was pulling on her socks.

"Good morning, sleepy head." Lexi gathered her up. "Shall we go see if Jethro is up?"

Jazi nodded.

But a quick trip through the suite revealed he'd already left for his office. A plate with toast crumbs and a coffee mug sat in the empty sink, evidence he'd had a little something to eat before he left.

A note on the counter reminded her of their appointment with the nursery manager at eleven. He asked her to notify Clay if she wanted to leave the hotel.

She frowned, suspecting she knew what that was about. But if Jethro thought she was taking a babysitter wherever she went, he had another think coming.

She'd soon find out because she wanted more than toast for breakfast.

"I hope you're hungry," she told Jazi while dressing her in gray knit pants and a lavender-and-gray shirt topped by a soft quilted vest in lavender. "I know a place that makes a great veggie omelet, but it's huge. You're going to have to eat your share."

"Hungry." Jazi nodded. "Jethro?"

"He's at work. It's just you and me, kid." The joy of that caused her hands to shake as she helped Jazi put on the black boots she'd chosen. She'd almost given up hope this day would come.

She remembered the look in Jethro's eyes last night and knew regret that her happiness came at his pain. She pushed the thought away. So it wasn't a perfect situation. The point was they were both doing what was best for Jazi.

That's what she needed to hold on to.

"The good news is there's plenty of time for us to go grocery shopping."

Jazi bounced up and down. "Shop!"

"You know that word, don't you? I think I'm in trouble."

Jazi giggled.

"Make that lots of trouble."

She called Clay and met him in the lobby. Jethro was with him along with a large, fit man in a dark suit.

Just as she feared, Jethro insisted she have a bodyguard when out in public. Hurt slammed into her like a kick to the stomach.

Forget it. She turned and walked away. She'd sit on her butt for three months before she let him make a puppet of her.

"Ms. Malone," he called out, her name a demand to stop and fall into line.

Yeah, right. Not. Going. To. Happen.

"Ms. Malone." He sounded closer.

She walked faster. The elevators were just ahead.

"Lexi, wait." He grabbed her arm and her own momentum swung her around.

She glared at his hand on her arm. "Let me go."

"Just listen to me."

She yanked at her arm. He released her instantly and she backed away. "I thought we agreed to respect each other. No puppets or puppies."

"This isn't about that." He blocked her path to the elevators. "This is about Jazi's safety, about your safety."

"Don't patronize me. Nothing is going to happen to us."

"I'm not willing to take a chance. I along with the other chief officers are worth millions. As long as you're with me, you're both targets."

"I can't." She pictured having to constantly account to someone for her movements and claustrophobia closed in on her. Shaking her head, she yanked at the collar of her sweater.

"Listen, this isn't public knowledge, last year Jackson was attacked and seriously injured in this hotel. It's only for three months," he reminded her, "and it will give me peace of mind."

"Jackson was hurt here in the hotel?" The shocking news got to Lexi where arguments would fail. "Okay."

Jethro escorted her back to where the men waited. Clay introduced the man with him as Damon Gregory, head of security for the casino and hotel. He'd accompany Lexi whenever Jethro or Clay couldn't.

"I don't know why you're doing this," Jethro stated as they walked through the supermarket doors. "I told you to make out a list and Brennan would order the groceries in."

"I like getting out." She helped Jazi into the seat of the cart. "And I like to do my own shopping. Especially this first time. It'll make me feel more at home in the kitchen. Is there anything you want me to add to the list?"

He stared at her for a moment. "I don't expect you to cook for me."

"Don't be ridiculous." She waved that away. "We live together. It only makes sense we eat the same meals. And it's just as easy to cook for three as two."

"I don't want to impose."

"Please." Imposing was asking her to move in for three months. "You're buying the food. You're welcome to whatever I make. So—" she pulled her list from her purse "—anything you want to add to the list?"

"I'm sure I'll like whatever you make."

"Then you get what you get." Honestly, the man's picture should be next to *difficult* in the dictionary. With her list in hand, she breezed through the aisles. Jethro worked on his phone the whole time. She said nothing when he tossed in a bag of chocolate cookies except to ask if there were any other sweet treats he liked. Without breaking off his conversation, he grabbed a bag of peanut butter sandwich cookies and added it to the cart.

Back at the hotel Jethro pulled in to the valet, instructed the captain to have the groceries delivered to his suite and escorted her inside, the package of chocolate cookies tucked under his arm.

"Was that so bad?" he quizzed her.

She wrinkled her nose at him.

The corner of his mouth crooked up at the end in a half smile. He yanked on her ponytail. "Try to give us at least a half hour notice when you want to go out. See you." And off he went.

"Not so bad," Lexi said to Jazi, "but still restricting. And we didn't encounter a single threat."

"Cookie?" Clearly Jazi had other priorities.

"Later, kiddo. We just ate."

The groceries would take a few minutes to get to the penthouse so Lexi stopped off at the Modern Goddess Spa to introduce Jazi to her friends. Of course everyone exclaimed how adorable she was. The little tyke loved the attention, especially when she got a cookie.

But the visit took a wicked turn when Maggie pinned Lexi with a knowing grin and demanded, "So you and Jethro Calder, hum? Spill, girl. I want details, vivid, leave-nothing-out details."

CHAPTER NINE

THE VISIT TO Modern Goddess lasted longer than Lexi planned. Her watch read ten-thirty when she carried Jazi into the suite. She and Jazi both needed freshening up so the groceries would have to wait. She planned to toss the perishables in the refrigerator and organize everything when she got back.

Except everything was already put away.

She set Jazi down and checked out the cupboards and refrigerator. "Okay, I could get used to this."

Jazi helped by opening one of the lower cabinets and pulling out pans until the door opened. "Jethro!" She ran to him and he swept her up. "Hi."

"Hello. It looks like someone got cake."

"A cookie actually." Lexi shoved the pan back in the cupboard and joined him in the foyer. "We were just headed in to get cleaned up. We'll be ready in a jiff."

He glanced at his watch as he handed over Jazi.

"Don't worry," Lexi reassured him. "We won't be late."

He lifted a skeptical brow.

Oh, challenge on. She had to forgo changing her clothes, but she added some color to her cheeks and a swipe of gloss to her lips. Jazi got a clean diaper, a dusting of powder and the soiled vest was replaced with a pretty sweater with bows on the shoulders.

Within ten minutes they were back in the foyer waiting on Jethro.

The meeting with Velveth turned out to be interesting. The hotel nannies were available twenty-four-seven, and could watch a child or children in the guests' room or in their care center which looked like a preschool with all its toys and amusements for the children. There were cribs and daybeds in a quiet chamber and a theater room for TV and movies. For older kids a media room held game consoles and computers with customized parental controls. There was a lounge and a play area.

All the rooms were monitored by cameras and two people manned the control room at all times.

From what Lexi saw, all the kids, from a one-year-old to a young teen, seemed to be having a good time. Jethro let her lead the appointment. She asked a few questions of Velveth and a few of the other nannies and she liked what she heard. If the need arose, she'd feel comfortable leaving Jazi in their care.

At the end of the appointment, Jethro thanked Velveth and escorted Lexi and Jazi out of the nursery.

"I have one more thing I want to show you." A warm hand in the small of her back directed her toward the casino.

He dropped his hand but stayed close through the casino. Just past the cashier cage, they came to a set of double doors discreetly marked Employees Only. A hallway led to a world she knew all too well, backstage of the theater.

Stagehands and crew members scurried about prepping the theater for the evening show. And from the sound of feet slapping wood, dancers were on stage rehearsing. Her senses absorbed the sights and sounds, the very beat of the world she'd left behind. It was a moment of comfort and angst.

Curiosity got the best of her. "What have you got up your sleeve, Jethro?"

He looked up from his phone. "You'll see. Here's Veronica now."

A woman swept toward them. Just shy of plump, she wore a colorful, flowing robe over a leotard and tights and her gray hair flowed over her shoulder in a thick braid. A beautiful bohemian.

Lexi recognized her immediately. Veronica Snow, choreographer of Pinnacle's dance production *Acropolis*. The woman had an Emmy, a Tony, and an Oscar.

"Jethro!" She claimed a kiss on the cheek. "How good to see you. You so rarely visit us."

"Ronnie, you'd never get anything done if you had to chase away all the men who'd like to spend time here."

She threw back her head in a hearty laugh. "This is true. But for the handsome four, we would make an exception."

Handsome four? It fit the Fabulous Four perfectly. Jethro had a fan.

Jazi stirred, disturbed by the talking. Lexi patted her back.

"Ronnie, this is the friend I was telling you about." Without asking Jethro lifted Jazi from her arms and settled her against his shoulder.

"Yes, I see. You didn't tell me it was Lexi Malone. How are you, dear? I've seen you dance. You're good, very good."

"Thank you. That means a lot coming from you. I truly admire your work." She stepped closer to Jethro to make room for a man carrying a large torch to get by.

"And I yours." Used to the hustle and bustle, Veronica ignored the activity. "You dance from the heart but hit every beat perfectly. Such musicality is a gift. If you're looking for work, there was no need to go through the usual channels. The answer is yes, we'd love to have you."

"Oh." Shocked and overjoyed, it was on the tip of Lexi's tongue to grab the offer. How she missed performing. But that wasn't her life anymore. She glanced at Jethro to gauge his reaction. Was this a test?

Was he hoping she'd choose dancing over Jazi, freeing him from his promise?

Not going to work. She loved dancing, but she loved Jazi more. And she'd promised Alliyah she'd take care of her.

His expression gave nothing away. After a moment, he lifted one dark eyebrow prompting a response.

Veronica Snow watched Lexi expectantly.

With the call of dancers pounding in the background it took all her will to say no.

She clasped her hands over her heart. "I'm very flattered. And I would honestly love to take you up on the offer, but I've given up performing. I'm a mother now. I need to be available during the day for Jazi's care."

"There is a wonderful nursery on-site here at the hotel. I'm sure we could work something into your contract."

Though it really did hurt to do so, she shook her head. "I'm afraid I have to refuse."

"So you really just want to practice?"

"Practice? I don't understand?"

Jethro spoke up. "I know you miss the dancing, so I asked Ronnie if you could have access to the practice room for exercise."

"Really?" The gesture overwhelmed Lexi. "That would be so perfect." She turned hopeful eyes on Veronica. "Would it be okay?"

Veronica's thick braid bobbed with her answer. "I think we can figure something out. I'll send you our practice schedule. You understand the process so you know I can't promise the practice room will be empty of dancers at any given point, but you are welcome to use the room."

"Right, someone is always wanting extra practice time. I promise to stay out of the way."

"It's agreed then." Veronica smiled. "I have to get back to work, but I hope we'll have the opportunity to get to know each other better."

"I'd like that." Lexi's feet itched to hit the boards, but it would have to wait until later. She held back until the other woman disappeared behind the curtains before throwing her arms around Jethro.

"Thank you." She hugged him and Jazi too. "Thank you.

Thank you." She pulled back, fought the urge to kiss him smack on the mouth. "This is the best thing anyone has ever done for me. It's so thoughtful of you."

"It's sheer self-preservation." He stepped back to soothe Jazi, who got jostled during the embrace.

"What do you mean?"

"I've seen you dance, Lexi. It's more than an occupation for you. It's an outlet. If you can't dance, you're likely to drive me crazy over the next three months."

"I likely will anyway." She hooked her arm through his for the walk out. "But maybe not as badly. And I'm too happy to care if the gesture has ulterior motives. Thank you."

He held the door open for her and relented a little. "A dancer should dance."

She nearly stumbled over her own feet. It was the nicest thing he'd ever said to her.

Lexi juggled two boxes of cupcakes and a balloon bouquet while trying to insert the key card for the suite. She held the card, she'd thought that far ahead, but she couldn't see what she was doing. Suddenly the door opened and she fell inward.

Jethro reacted quickly, stepping forward to block her fall and catch the boxes. He did a quick juggling act of his own and his arm ended up around her waist and she ended up pressed to his side while he easily handled the two boxes with one hand on the bottom.

For the first time in her life she knew what it meant to swoon. Cradled against him, admiring his quick reflexes and agile movements, while surrounded by his strength and warmth, inhaling the sexy musk of man and soap, she just wanted to melt into him.

Control, Lexi, no jumping the man and burying your nose in his neck.

Instead she pulled away from his support.

"Whoa. Good catch." She let him take the boxes, watched as he set them on the foyer table. "I wasn't expecting you for a while or I would have knocked."

"My meeting wrapped early." He looked handsome as ever in his black pants and white shirt. And as reserved. She followed as he returned to the living room. A big pink box sat on the coffee table. He sat down and picked up a big white bow.

"Good. I can use the help. I'm running a little late." She grabbed a couple of bags from the corner and brought them over. She dropped to the floor across from him and started pulling things from the bags. "I still need to wrap my gifts." She hesitated. "I'm so glad you could be a part of the party."

"It's likely the only birthday I'll spend with her."

Yeah, she hadn't wanted to mention that.

"She'll be thrilled." His words were matter-of-fact so she should take them that way and move on. Except she couldn't. If he was only going to get this one birthday with his daughter, it should consist of more than a party in the nursery surrounded by noisy kids and employees. "I'm going to take her to the arcade for dinner. You're welcome to join us if you want."

"I'll have to see how my schedule looks later."

"Of course." Gathering the balloons floating about the foyer, she anchored them before following him into the living room.

"What's in the box?"

"You'll have to wait and see."

"Okay, be that way, then."

He frowned, eyed her uncertainly. Poor baby. She really shouldn't tease, but she'd never met anyone who needed it more. He took life way too seriously.

"Well, I got her an animated movie. A baby doll with clothes. And a bag of plastic building blocks. When you're done putting your bow on, you can help wrap mine."

"Wrapping really isn't my thing."

"You're doing a great job. And I have bags for mine. You just drop the gift in, put tissue paper on top and you're done. Thank you by the way."

"For what?"

"Authorizing the party. I get the feeling Velveth would have been a lot less cooperative if not for you."

"Having it in the nursery was a smart choice."

"Right? Instant party. Which is perfect for this year. Velveth had a few concerns. Thanks for smoothing the way there. I talked to her a few minutes ago. She's getting parent consent forms as kids are dropped off. Nobody has objected and luckily none of the kids so far have allergies, so she's happy.

"I'll confess I'm glad there will be staff to help with this party. I'm still too new at this mothering thing to be comfortable wrangling a dozen kids."

"I'm sure you'll be fine. You must have plenty of experience with birthday parties."

"Not as much as you think." She focused on the cupcake tower she was assembling. "When my dad was alive he made the whole day special and there was always a big cake with buttercream icing." She licked her lips. "Best icing ever. But when it was just mom and me, it was just dinner out and a birthday sundae. What about you?"

"I wasn't really into celebrating my birthday. Most of the foster families respected that."

"Well, that's sad." She was curious but did not push for more information. She didn't care to expound on her history so she'd give him the same courtesy.

"Mama Harman felt the same way."

"That's the home where you met Jackson, Ryan and Clay?"

"Yeah. She felt life was to be celebrated. She had a tradition for birthdays where she cooked the birthday boy's favorite meal and baked a cake. I was to be no different."

"It sounds like a nice tradition."

"Yes, well the other guys wanted cake, so I went along with it. She made me a present."

"The cap in your closet."

He arched a dark brow at her. Sheepish, she smiled and shrugged.

"It's all I have left from her." Rather than look at her he opened the biggest gift bag and dropped in the blocks.

"She must have been a remarkable woman to take on the four of you."

"There would be no Fabulous Four without her influence."

Mangled tissue topped the gift. Lexi let it go, more concerned with him than his wrapping skills. When he reached for the next bag, she laid her hand over his. "Then the world is truly a better place because of her."

He did look at her then, undefinable emotion darkening his eyes. He nodded. "Thank you."

"Mr. Calder, Lexi, hello," Velveth greeted them. "We got the cart you sent down and we are ready for you." She led them to the meal room where they'd pushed several tables together to make a square big enough for all the kids to sit around.

"This is perfect," Lexi exclaimed. They'd set up a festive table with the party items she sent down. She'd chosen a fish theme in honor of Jazi's favorite book. The cupcakes served as a centerpiece and favor bags waited at each seat.

"Thanks for letting us have the party here."

"We are pleased to be of service," Velveth replied, her gaze sliding toward Jethro. "Shall we call the children?"

"I'm ready if you are." Lexi wandered over to where Jethro leaned against a work counter.

She copied his stance, waiting to see Jazi's expression.

Velveth returned, ushering children ahead of her. Jazi's eyes were huge with wonder and excitement. Lexi snapped a picture.

The kids ranged in age from one to twelve. Three staff members helped to get them settled at the table. The older ones dug into the favor bags, while the younger ones looked at the tower of cupcakes with awe.

Lexi took the top cupcake with the two candles and placed it in front of the little girl. Lexi lit the candles. Everyone sang "Happy Birthday."

The best part, Jazi's grin reached ear to ear. She picked up her cupcake and began to lick off the chocolate icing. Grabbing two from the display, Lexi carried them to Jethro.

"Chocolate or vanilla?" She held one out on each palm. He took the chocolate.

"Time for presents," Velveth announced.

Lexi got her gifts and Jazi tore through them. She insisted on opening the baby doll and hugged it to her. Lexi tucked the clothes away and promised Jazi they'd play with the blocks later. She pointed at the big pink box. Jethro brought it over.

Lexi bent over Jazi and helped her remove the lid.

"Bow!" Jazi exclaimed.

OMG. He'd got her a fish.

Later that evening in the arcade Lexi chuckled at Jazi's antics. Frustrated by the fact the skeet ball kept rolling back, she climbed up on the ball alley and walked it up to drop it in the hole. Then she came back for the next one.

Lexi glanced around to see if they were about to be busted and spied Jethro propping up a column about ten feet away. She waved him over, but he shook his head.

Oh, for heaven's sake. She tended to Jazi, helping her by tossing in a couple of balls, then she gathered her up.

But when Lexi turned around, Jethro was gone.

Lexi came slowly awake. She pushed back the covers and went to the bathroom. Since she was up, she grabbed her robe off the armchair and decided to check on Jazi. They'd been with Jethro ten days now and thankfully there'd been no screaming fits. But Jazi still tended to wander at night.

Sometimes she made her way into Lexi's room and crawled into bed with her. But Lexi had found her in the living room, the media room and, one unforgettable time, under her bed.

Sure enough Jazi's covers were mussed and the girl was missing.

Lexi went looking, and the more she searched the more unnerved she became. She couldn't find her anywhere, not even under her bed. Nothing.

Fear beating through her she headed down the hall. Time to wake up Jethro. It was only when she got close to his door and found it open that she realized Jazi had sought out her father. She slept on her back, arms flung out and he slept on his side half curled around her, one bare shoulder exposed so his hand could rest on her lower leg.

Father and daughter sleeping so peacefully together.

Seeing them together like this made Lexi question her whole plan.

And her distress shifted in a whole new direction. Was she being selfish in wanting to provide a loving family for Jazi when her real family was right here? This was her father. She'd taken to him from their very first meeting. She ran to him whenever he got home. And he always handled her with such gentleness.

He should have taken more time to think before he agreed to Lexi's proposition.

He said he didn't know anything about raising a child, but he cared. He might feel out of his depth raising a little girl, but there was no denying he cared about Jazi. Lexi wouldn't be here if he didn't.

Her gut clenched as her heartbeat went wild. Because the Lord knew she wasn't any better qualified. All she had in her favor was love.

But she also knew with Jethro's affection and a good nanny Jazi would be set.

But he had promised, and Lexi had her vow to Alliyah to honor. Even if she could bring herself to give Jazi up, she owed Alliyah more than she could ever give back. Raising Jazi into a woman her mother would be proud of was the only way left to show gratitude to the woman who'd saved her soul.

Lexi began to back out of the room.

"You should take her back to bed." A husky male voice broke the silence.

Lexi froze, mortified to be caught hovering in his room. Had she given herself away, made a distressed sound to awaken him?

No other choice but to brazen it through.

She went to the bed and gathered Jazi into her arms. Avoiding his gaze, she said, "I'm sorry she bothered you."

"It's still a new place for her. She'll settle in. It's been several days since her last visit."

The rasp in his voice touched her on a visceral level so she almost missed the message in the words.

"You mean this isn't the first time?"

"No. The first time I found her curled up outside my door." He raised up on his elbow and the covers dropped to the bed revealing his muscular chest. Thank goodness for the darkness. "After that I left the door ajar. This is the second time she's climbed into bed with me."

"I'm sorry," she repeated, cuddling the girl close. So the nights Lexi thought she'd slept through, she'd been with Jethro.

"You too?"

"Yes. And I've found her in other places in the suite. I was happy she'd slept a few nights in her own bed, but I guess she was with you. Maybe I should just let her sleep with me."

He shook his head. "I can't think that's a good habit to

start. She's just learning her environment on her own terms. She'll settle down."

"Okay." Time stretched out and Lexi realized she was staring, admiring the way the dim light curved over his muscles. Heat rushed to her cheeks. What an odd night. "Well," she cleared the rasp from her throat, "good night."

"Hey, Lexi?" He stopped her flight from the room.

"Yes." She paused one foot out the door.

"I have an early meeting—" he ran a hand through his already ruffled hair,"—but I wanted to ask if you'll be my concubine tonight?"

She blinked. Concubine?

"There's this charity thing tonight, and—"

"You need a date." She broke in when her brain caught up with the conversation.

"Yes. As we are living together—"

"Of course I'll go with you." Anything to get out of this room and away from the sight of him all sleep rumpled and wrapped in nothing more than a sheet. Sexy much? More than she could handle at three in the morning. "What should I wear?"

"It's a costume deal. I'll have my assistant send you the details."

"Okay. But just so you know, I don't put out on the third nondate." Holding Jazi close, she fled from the room.

CHAPTER TEN

THE INFORMATION CAME along with costumes. The note said the charity event for diabetes started at eight in Pinnacle's high-stakes casino, Sky Tower. The four top executives of Pinnacle would be attending as characters from the game. They'd be battle chiefs and their dates: concubines.

Battle chiefs were like chieftains, their status gained by the number of their kills, and concubines were their lethal mistresses.

Fun. Lexi dug into the first garment bag and found Jethro's battle chief costume, a cross between a modern-day biker and an Old West gunslinger. OMG, with his austere persona and dark good looks he'd look like he walked right out of the game. In fact, the fab four were going to be smokin' hot tonight.

The concubine costume, on the other hand, lacked...a lot, including material. She'd look like a Goth Tinkerbell in the dark green strapless number. And she'd be lucky if the hemline covered the essentials. As a dancer, Lexi was used to skimpy—this dress might work in a video game where it was painted on, but she preferred not to flash the world.

Especially while accompanying Jethro.

Luckily, she knew just what to do.

Jethro pulled on the leather duster that completed his costume and shrugged it into place. The air-conditioning better be cranked up in the Sky Tower or he'd be sweating inside an hour.

At least the black jeans and tee underneath were comfortable. If he didn't count the ammo strapped over his chest or the guns on his hips. Hopefully, he wouldn't have to stay long.

"Hi, lover. I'm ready."

He swung around. And about swallowed his tongue.

Lexi stood propped against the doorjamb squeezed into a green number that clung to every soft curve. She wore black thigh-high boots, black stockings and a knife strapped to her thigh. A leather jacket was hooked over one pale, bare shoulder.

Her beautiful features shimmered under an incandescent makeup, making her eyes huge and her lips a kissable cherry red. All of it framed by an intricate upswept do that ended in a fall of curls over her left shoulder.

So sexy he took a step toward her.

"Lexi." He pulled himself to a stop. "You look stunning."

The compliment earned him a delighted grin. "And you look like a bad boy."

"Then I'd say we're ready to go." He relaxed into the leather feeling less of a fraud. He could be a bad boy when necessary. He offered her his arm. "Shall we?"

She hooked her hand around his elbow. Heck, with her by his side people probably wouldn't even notice him. They'd be too busy eying her.

Instead of going down and across to the other elevators, he swiped his key card and hit the button for the top floor. The doors opened into a luxurious lounge refitted to a banquet room complete with dance floor. Dim lighting provided discretion while a domed glass ceiling and walls displayed the best view in Las Vegas.

Music from the party grew louder as Jethro led Lexi past the bar to the casino. As requested they were early so the casino was empty except for the band and waitstaff.

The ten-thousand-dollar tickets gained the attendee access to the casino where there was an open bar and five food stations, each with a different international theme.

Later there'd be dancing and a raffle. The extravagant gifts included a week's stay at any Pinnacle resort.

A rep from the charity spotted him and came running over. "Mr. Calder, good evening, sir. I'm Clark. Thank you so much for your participation in tonight's event. May I say you both look spectacular?"

Taking that as a rhetorical question, Jethro waited for the plump gentleman in the Mongol costume to direct them where to go.

"Thank you." Lexi spoke into the silence. "We're looking forward to the event. I hope you meet your goal tonight."

"Oh, my." The man clasped his clipboard to his thread-bare tunic. "Haven't you heard? We sold out. Every ticket. And OMG, we got so many calls asking for exceptions. This is going to be the event of the year. And it's all thanks to Pinnacle."

"Glad we could help." Not liking the way the man's gaze lingered on Lexi, Jethro drew her closer to his side. "Where do you need us?"

"Yes, of course. This way please. The doors will open momentarily. We'd like for the executives to greet the guests as they enter. Mr. Hawke is already here."

"Jethro." Jackson greeted him by pounding his back. "Best gala ever."

"I'm sure you think so." Jackson's outfit resembled Jethro's except he wore khakis and had a sword strapped over his leather duster. "Grace, you look lovely. You bring an elegance to the concubine they could never duplicate in the game."

"Thanks," the tall black-haired woman sheathed in a silver concubine dress responded. "That's because I had them add four inches."

Lexi laughed. "Smart."

"You must be the mysterious Lexi. I'm Grace, Jackson's fiancée."

"More temporary than mysterious. It's nice to meet you." Lexi shook her hand.

"Oh, how sweet of you. He hasn't mentioned me has he?" Grace sent Jethro a chiding sidelong look. "He's been very closedmouthed about you and Jasmine."

"And that's not going to change tonight." A pinch on his side revealed Lexi's displeasure. He ignored her. "Here come Clay and Ryan."

Both men had beautiful women on their arms, the concubine dresses clinging to ripe curves. Quick introductions were made and then the doors were opened allowing in the swarm of guests. The next hour flew by. The costumes were varied and inventive, the guests engaged and friendly.

And the soft scent of tropical blooms reminded him of the woman by his side.

When the line began to thin, she leaned close and whispered, "I'm starved."

"Me too. Let's ditch this. We've done our duty."

Across the way Ryan tilted his head indicating they were cutting out too.

Jethro followed the group to the Italian station. Lagging back a bit he leaned down to Lexi. "We have a reserved table so we'll join the others to eat, but I expect you to respect my privacy."

She patted his arm. "Yeah, I got the message. Don't worry. Your secrets are safe with me."

Funny, he actually trusted her. And because he did, dinner turned out to be fun. He had to block two attempts by Grace to get Lexi alone, but he relaxed after Grace groused that he needn't bother, Lexi wasn't dishing any dirt.

Clark appeared at the table asking for the executives to pose for a group picture.

Jethro stood along with his friends and reached for his jacket. "At least the air is flowing up here."

"You're welcome." Clay shrugged into his duster. "I

called housekeeping as soon as I put this thing on tonight. Told them to crank up the AC."

Jackson clapped him on the shoulder. "We can always rely on you to handle the details regarding our comfort."

"Damn straight."

The photographer was set up near an internal 3-D wall depicting the ruins of a city. He arranged them—some standing, some crouching in the ruins—and began taking pictures. Behind him people gathered, taking photos with their phones. They must be a sight—this was not a group easily impressed. Jethro saw Lexi with her phone out and shook his head.

"Enough." He broke pose to a round of groans. Jackson enjoyed this stuff, let him stay and work the crowd.

Grabbing Lexi's hand, Jethro pushed through the throng of people headed for the lounge.

"Where are we going?"

"I thought you might like to dance." This night was not ending before he held her in his arms. One dance and he'd be ready to leave.

The band just started a moody ballad as he reached the lounge. He ditched the duster then took her hand and drew her onto the dance floor. Pulling her close, he moved into a smooth waltz.

After a moment her head went back and she grinned up at him. "You're very good."

"Such surprise." He twirled her, led her through two steps and twirled her again.

She laughed her delight. "Try shock. I never had you pegged as a dancer."

"Tsk-tsk. That's shoddy research, Ms. Malone. I quite enjoy the occasional dance."

She wiggled well—defined eyebrows at him. "Meaning you like holding a beautiful woman in your arms to music."

His turn to laugh. "You've got me there."

The music changed to a slightly faster tune. He flawlessly shifted to a fox-trot. All grace, Lexi kept pace with him step for step. One more dance wouldn't hurt.

"When Mr. Harman was alive, Mama Harman was a ballroom dancer. It's a well-kept secret between the four of us that she taught us how to dance. She insisted we'd be happy she did. She was right."

Another secret revealed. This woman was entirely too easy to share with. Perhaps it was the way she spoke to him, as an equal, even teasing him sometimes when so many were intimidated by him.

"Besides being a closet dancer, what else do you do for fun?"

"Fun?"

"Yes, fun. You know, for recreation."

"I know what fun is, Ms. Malone." He lowered her into a dip.

"Do you? You seemed confused."

Not confused, surprised. People rarely concerned themselves with his amusements. "I like to read. I do some climbing, some sailing."

She eyed him suspiciously. "Please tell me you don't climb alone."

How was it she could read him so easily? A better question might be why did she care?

"I'm touched you care. But you needn't worry. I have a few climbing buddies. We keep each other safe."

"You're very insular, aren't you?" The music slowed again, and she looped her arms around his neck and swayed against him.

"I enjoy my own company." His hands went to her waist, so small he almost spanned it with his fingers.

"Right, it's quite safe isn't it?" she challenged softly.

"I'm a numbers man, Ms. Malone. I believe in playing it safe."

"Do you suppose you'll ever call me Lexi again?"

"Not likely."

"Why not?" Her lush cherry-red lips pursed in a pout.

Temptation pulled at him to lean down and taste the sweetness he knew matched the fruity color she'd painted those pretty lips. Instead he stepped back, ending the dance.

"It's safer this way."

"Hey, Lex." Jessica hailed her from the practice room doorway. "I'm sorry, but I have to bail on you. Toothache. My dentist has an opening so I grabbed it."

"No problem, Jess." Lexi walked toward the tall blonde. She knew Jessica from the Golden Cuff. She'd left to go to the Pinnacle just before Alliyah's accident.

Lexi had been thrilled when Jessica had asked her to help her choreograph an audition number for an upcoming show. It allowed her to dip her toe back into dancing during daylight hours. It was a little bittersweet to start out, because she was used to being the performer, but watching Jessica master the piece filled her with satisfaction and pride.

"Best to take care of it or you'll feel it when you're dancing."

"Yeah, I found that out. Listen, I gave up my time in the practice room, but I'm sure the girls would be happy to share with you. I've had three people ask if you're taking on additional clients."

"Clients?" Lexi laughed. "You're my friend. I'm only taking your money because you insisted."

"And you're worth more than I'm paying." Jessica checked her watch. "I've got to go, but we're definitely on for Thursday. Oh, and I almost forgot—Veronica asked if you'd stop by her office."

Really? "Thanks for letting me know. Good luck at the dentist."

Jessica waved on her way out the door and Lexi went to gather her gear, wondering what Veronica wanted to see her about. She found the older woman in her office adjacent to the practice room. The office was good-sized with a huge old-fashioned teacher's desk, a chaise longue in the corner and two plum-colored visitor chairs.

Lexi knocked on the open door.

"Give me a minute." Gray head bent, Veronica's hands and fingers moved to unheard music as she flipped through a document on the tablet in front of her. She shook her head once, made a change then nodded and set the tablet aside. Only then did she look up.

"Lexi," the choreographer exclaimed, "come in. Thanks for coming by." She rose and indicated for Lexi to take one of the visitor chairs. "Sorry about that." She waved at the desk as she sat in the second chair. "I'm working on a new dance and I had to get the sequence down while it was fresh in my head."

"No problem. We have to respect the process, don't we?"

"Exactly." Veronica clapped her hands and beamed at Lexi as if she'd performed a wondrous feat. "That's one of the things I like most about you, Lexi, you respect the process and it shows. You take what's given to you and make it your own, bringing a refinement to the work so it appears effortless no matter how grueling the piece is."

Lexi flushed with pleasure. "That's quite a compliment coming from you."

"Believe me, I'm not the only one to notice." Veronica turned in the chair to face Lexi, leaning forward solicitously. "It's the very reason I want to talk to you."

"Really?" Curiosity drew Lexi to the edge of her seat.

"Yes. I'd like for you to consult with me on this new dance."

"Consult?" The word came out as a squeal. Shock could do that to a woman. Lexi felt her eyes pop wide and blinked to gain control. "Me?"

"Don't be so surprised. As I said, your talent has been noticed. I've also seen the improvement in Jessica's dancing since you've been working with her. You've earned this."

"Wow, thank you. I would absolutely love to work with

you. Please know that right up front. But what kind of time commitment would you want? I have Jazi to care for." She'd come too close to losing her daughter not to put her needs first, no matter how fabulous the offer.

"Of course." Veronica reached out and patted Lexi's hand. "It shouldn't require more than a few hours a day a couple of times a week. Frankly, at this point that's all the time I have to put into it. It'll pick up once we start practice, but I'm willing to work with you."

"This is such a surprise." Lexi shook with excitement. She'd have been happy to dance for the woman, having the opportunity to work with her blew Lexi's mind. "Let me talk to Jethro." Okay, she never thought she'd say those words. But he was her partner, of sorts, for the time being. "If he has no objections, I'm in a hundred percent."

"Wonderful. I can't expect he will." Veronica stood. When Lexi also stood, the other woman enveloped her in a fragrant hug. "I'm so excited to be working with you. Call me after you talk to Jethro and we'll set up a schedule."

Lexi's head was still reeling when she reached the penthouse. The unexpected sound of voices coming from the living room drew her in that direction. She blinked at the crowd of strangers sprawled throughout the room. Several held instruments and everyone seemed to be talking at the same time.

A shrill whistle cut through the din and one voice drawled, "Well, hello, sweet thing, who might you be?"

The man had warm brown eyes, dark hair and a trim beard. He looked familiar.

Warm hands cupped her shoulders. "This is Lexi Malone." Jethro stood from behind her. "She lives with me." The message was clearly a hands-off warning. Lexi wasn't sure how she felt about that. But he went on. "Lexi, this is—"

"Jack Rabbits," she finished for him. The crowd turned

out to be two men and two women and one of country music's up-and-coming bands. This was turning out to be quite a day.

"Yes. Pinnacle has just signed them to our label and they were going to show me their new song. I thought you might enjoy sitting in. We can go somewhere else if you prefer."

"No, no. I'd love to sit in." She faced their company. "If it's okay with you? I love your music."

"It's fine with us." The bearded man flashed a friendly grin.

"Fans are always welcome. Hi, Lexi." A slim redhead stepped forward to shake her hand. "I'm Holly. And this is Nathan, Roy and Kate. We're never happier than when we have an audience."

"Goody." She clapped her hands, not even caring she was acting like a teenage girl. Still she made an effort to pull herself together. "Did Jethro offer you refreshments?

"Thank you. We just came from lunch." Holly spoke for the group. "Now we're eager to sing our song for Jethro."

"Then let's get started." Jethro took charge.

Soon the band was situated on the sofa, with Roy in a dining room chair at the end to give him more room to play his guitar. Jethro offered her the chair but she dropped to the carpet next to him and sat cross-legged. She'd left her phone with her gear in the foyer so she glanced up at Jethro. "Can you let the nursery know I'll be late picking up Jazi?"

In response, he pulled out his phone and sent a text. Then he nodded to Roy. "Whenever you're ready."

"We'll start with a couple of our hits if you don't mind." Roy strummed the strings of his guitar. "Singing something familiar helps to warm us up."

He began the chords to "Sunshine and Roses," one of Lexi's favorites. She started to sing along and covered her mouth to stop herself, but a nod from Kate told her it was okay. With a grin she joined in.

For all Lexi's years of studying music, she'd never participated in a jam session. She rocked to the beat as the music flowed through her. This felt like a rite of passage in some ways. So much fun, she couldn't stop smiling.

After a couple of songs, Roy began to pick a slower tune.

"We're still working out some of the harmonies," Holly warned them. "But we think this has the potential to go to number one on the charts."

Lexi hugged her knees as the band began to sing. The song portrayed a single mother learning to trust in love again. It was a lovely ballad with a heartfelt chorus.

When the band finished, they started discussing the harmony changes they were considering. Lexi heard the same stresses they did and she longed to share her ideas, but it wasn't her place. She pressed her lips together and listened.

Jethro sat back and observed. The song was good. He agreed with the potential the band predicted. It sounded fine to him, but the band all agreed something in the chorus needed fixing, they just didn't agree on what.

The corner of his mouth ticked up when his gaze moved to Lexi. She sat at his feet practically vibrating with the need to join the conversation. He appreciated her discretion—the band probably wouldn't appreciate her unsolicited advice. On the other hand as one of the owners, he had more leeway.

"Lexi, what do you think?"

All chatter stopped and five sets of eyes landed on him.

"She has a doctorate in music," he said easily. "I've never met anyone with a finer ear."

The band members looked at each other and then at Lexi. She sent him a glance that was half accusation half gratitude.

"I do have a couple of suggestions, if you're interested," she offered.

"Sure." Nathan spoke for the group. "We don't promise to use them, but we're willing to listen."

"The transition you're stumbling over might benefit from a change of a two-syllable word over a three-syllable word, maybe *tough* instead of *difficult*. Something that simple can give you the extra beat you're missing. I also thought it might add a spark of interest to speed the chorus up a few of beats."

The band's reaction was a mix of thoughtful and skeptical. To demonstrate Lexi began to sing. She had a few pitch problems but overall she recalled the lyrics of the first refrain and nailed the chorus. Before she finished, the band was nodding and they jumped in and continued the song.

At the end they all started talking at once, excitedly drawing Lexi into the conversation. Holly whipped out a tablet and noted changes. She passed the device along and each member of the band nodded.

"Let's try it one more time." Roy played the opening chords.

At Jethro's feet Lexi closed her eyes, her fingers tapping to the beat. A serene smile lifted the corners of her mouth. He heard the difference too, and nodded. He preferred not to contemplate the fact he took almost as much satisfaction in her joy as in the betterment of the song.

As the last verse faded away, a hushed silence filled the room.

Nathan jumped to his feet with a whoop, his fist punched to the ceiling in triumph. "That was sweet, sweet music." He stepped around the coffee table and swept Lexi up into a big hug. "Now it's a number one."

Jethro tensed, ready to intercede. But he was the only one uncomfortable. She laughed and hugged the big, barrel-chested man. Then she went on to hug the rest of the band. Jethro relaxed back in his chair until Holly came over and demanded a hug. Maybe he was the one who needed saving.

He survived it, barely, egged on by Lexi's teasing smile. Still he breathed easier when the band announced they needed to leave for their next engagement. "I'll walk you out."

Unsettled with himself—he never got jealous—he wandered back into the room and suddenly found his arms full of warm woman.

"Thank you. Thank you. Thank you." She nearly strangled him in her enthusiasm and still he pulled her closer. It had been too long since he'd felt a woman's curves against his body. Too soon she pulled away. He suffered a kiss on the cheek.

"It was so sweet of you to include me." She hooked her elbow around his and led him back to the living room. "This has been the best day ever. Let me get you a drink and I'll tell you about the offer Veronica made me."

"Don't tell me you're joining the troupe?" Now there was a temptation he'd find hard to resist.

"Even better, she wants me to choreograph a dance with her."

Lexi poured a glass of chardonnay and carried it along with the baby monitor to a comfortable chair in the living room. She set down the baby monitor and used a remote to open the drapes to the fabulous view. She put on an album by one of her all-time-favorite female artists and turned the volume down low. With a sigh, she sank into the soft cushions and took her first sip. Nice. Peace at last.

Jazi finally slept. She'd been a handful tonight as she'd been cranky from the lack of a nap. Jethro was out at a dinner meeting.

Another week down. That made three.

A second sip made it easy to admit it hadn't been that bad.

In fact, time flew by. She loved all the Jazi time. And after the first week, she'd settled into a rhythm. Unless he had an early meeting, Jethro ate breakfast with them. He joined them for dinner three or four times a week though he checked in with her several times a day.

In the morning she taught Jazi baby yoga and read to her or they played songs on Lexi's electric piano. Mostly that meant she made up songs while Jazi played with her toys. She'd actually started composing a lullaby she really liked. Jazi liked it too. It put her to sleep almost every time. Tonight was the first time it had failed.

Jazi liked to go to the nursery in the afternoon. Time Lexi took advantage of to get in a dance workout or work with Jess or Veronica. Then it was back to the suite where Lexi put Jazi down for a nap while she started dinner.

Something she never expected from this arrangement was a resurgence of her dancing career. She loved working with Veronica choreographing a piece with multiple dancers. It was bigger and more challenging than anything she'd done to date.

And it was all due to Jethro.

She didn't know how to feel about that, so she didn't dwell on it. Surprisingly, he managed to be present without being obtrusive.

The one thing they clashed on was Jazi's bedtime. Lexi had a more open policy. She put Jazi down between eight and eight thirty every night, but if she didn't stay down, Lexi let her stay up until she'd tired herself out. Part of that was fear of the screaming fits coming back and part came from Lexi's determination not to force the restrictions on Jazi that she'd had forced on her.

Jethro believed Jazi should have a set bedtime that was enforced. He stated children craved structure and discipline and that required a set schedule.

She didn't totally disagree—she felt love, affection and a semiset schedule provided a sound foundation for Jazi without stifling her creativity and individuality. It wouldn't be an issue except for Jazi's little jaunts in the middle of the night. So Lexi was trying to set a schedule. Obviously there'd be a learning curve.

The only true blot so far was having to be escorted anytime she went out with Jazi. Clay generally took her wherever she needed to go. He never rushed her or acted as if the trip was unwarranted. And still she felt diminished and claustrophobic.

She felt like she was a teenager again and back under her mother's control. Mother never let Lexi have any independence. She always had to have friends, classmates, teachers or someone with her wherever she went, as if she didn't have the intelligence to be let out alone.

The lack of freedom and refusal to let her have dance in her life was what drove Lexi to leave home as soon as she turned eighteen. She felt sad over the way she left but she never regretted her decision.

She kept telling herself it was only three months—less now—but it didn't help. Something had to give, and it was Jethro.

Today she asked Clay what would change Jethro's mind about her having an escort and his response had been, *Nothing*.

Lexi didn't accept that.

She relaxed a little when Clay added, "He'd have bodyguards on the three of us if he had his way. Only the fact we'd insist he have one too keeps us safe from his overprotectiveness. But I won't lie—I sustain a high level of security on the executive floors, both office and sleeping. And I'm personally overseeing the security at Jackson's new house."

Okay, she understood a lot of money equaled a lot of risk. And it helped knowing she wasn't the only one that needed to take care. She still didn't like it.

Because more than her itchiness bothered Lexi. If Jethro truly feared for Jazi's safety and Lexi's ability to keep her from harm, would he use that as an excuse to keep her?

Everything she'd read and come to know about Jethro revealed him as an honorable man. Severe at times, but honorable. The only thing that trumped honor was loyalty. She could see him justifying breaking his word if he convinced himself it was in Jazi's best interest.

After all, that was his only reason for giving her up.

Which meant she needed to find a way to protect Jazi from harm. A smile slowly bloomed inside her and she uncurled to fetch her phone. She sent Clay a text and then toasted her brilliant idea and finished her wine.

Lexi slowly came awake. Eyes closed, she took stock of what she remembered. Man, the wine really knocked her out. She stretched her body, turning one way and then the other moaning softly as she worked out the kinks of slumbering in a chair.

She blinked her eyes open. A man loomed over her.

"Eee!" she screamed, pushing back in her chair to get away.

And then she was on her feet, fist flying. She had a daughter to protect.

In the next instant she recognized Jethro. He caught her hand in his, pulled her off-balance, swung her around and wrapped her in his arms. It happened so fast her head spun and she may have screamed again.

"Let go," she demanded, wiggling to be set free.

"It's Jethro," he said, his breath warm against her ear.

"Yeah, I figured it out." She tried twisting side to side, but found no give in his strong arms. "After you nearly scared me to death."

"I live here," he pointed out. "Who else would it be?"

"Oh, I don't know, assassins, kidnappers, zombies? Whatever else you believe can make off with Jazi or me."

"You're spooked. Is that why you want Clay to give you self-defense lessons?"

"I'm not spooked."

She stopped her efforts to be released. All she'd succeeded in doing was rubbing her body against his, which she liked way too much. And it distracted her from arguing with him. Holy tomatoes he smelled good.

"You're the one who is spooked. I freaked out because I woke up to find a strange man standing over me."

"I'm not strange."

"That's debatable."

"I meant I'm not a stranger."

"That's debatable too. Are you going to let me go or should we put music on and dance?"

She felt an odd shaking behind her and glared at him over her shoulder. "Are you laughing at me?"

"Would you hate me if I was?"

That made her stop and think. "No. But only because you don't laugh enough. Are you going to release me anytime soon?"

"I like you where you are."

She sucked in a breath. So he felt it too. The awareness between them that never really went away. The heat and sizzle that caused her skin to tingle whenever he was close. Like now.

"All the more reason you should."

"You're right, of course." And still he held her.

After a moment, his grip loosened and she forced herself to step away. She needed more wine. She picked up her glass and held it up. "Want a glass?"

"Sure." He followed her to the kitchen. "Zombies?" he asked.

She shrugged expressively. "It seems as likely as the other options."

"The other options are viable threats. I have letters to prove it."

"OMG." She handed him his wine. "You have letters threatening you? Why?"

He sipped his wine, hummed his approval. "I don't explain the crazies. I take steps against them." He gestured to her with the glass. "If you're not spooked, why do you want Clay to teach you self-defense?"

She carried her glass back to the living room, but his

question riled her too much to sit. "Because I feel like a delinquent teenager whenever I go out of the hotel. If I know
how to defend myself, and Jazi, then you won't have to send
an escort with us every time we leave the casino grounds."

He shook his head. "You won't be proficient enough in
two months to be effective."

"I might surprise you. I'm a dancer, which makes some
men think I'm easy." She flexed her biceps. "I've learned
to handle myself."

"Really?" He cocked a brow. "Because you'd have broken your thumb if you'd landed that punch."

She frowned. "Okay, I forgot about the thumb. I just need
a refresher on some things." Getting into the mood, she
bounced on her toes. "But I'm light on my feet and a quick
study. You'll be surprised at what I can learn in a month
when I'm motivated."

"Okay." He shrugged out of his jacket, tossed it over the
sofa. "Let's see what you've got." He pushed the sofa back
and then picked up the ottoman and carried it into the foyer.

"What?" She landed flat on her feet. "Now? Right here?"

"Yes." He moved her to the middle of the room and
shoved the chair back against the wall. After shifting a
couple more items out of the way, he faced her. "Here. Now."
He curled his fingers at her. "Come at me?"

Narrowing her eyes, she looked him over. She was awake
now and thinking clearly. He wanted to see her moves?
She'd show him.

The black yoga pants she wore along with an oversize tee
over a white tank were perfect for this exercise.

Bouncing on her toes, she shook out her whole body,
arms, fingers, legs. And then she bent at the waist and
stretched, keeping her legs straight as she touched her toes.
Next she turned her back to him and spread her legs a bit,
stretching down to touch her right foot, then up, and down
to her left foot. A peek between her legs showed an upside-

down version of Jethro with his feet shoulder-width apart and arms crossed over his chest.

But, oh, yeah, he was watching her butt.

Just the distraction she wanted.

"Are we going to do this tonight?" he demanded.

"Just loosening up," she responded. She faced him again and drew the oversize tee off over her head. His dark gaze zeroed in on her unfettered breasts. Normally she'd want a bra for any workout. Tonight, it worked to her advantage not to have one. Or so she hoped. "I don't want to strain anything."

Tossing the tee on the floor behind her, she did a few more stretches, twisting at the waist to the left and then the right, watching Jethro' eyes follow the movements. Now she was ready.

She prowled across the room, slowly approaching him. "So you want to tangle?" she asked, her voice breathy. All soft curves and subtle hip action, she moved closer, invading his space to whisper in his ear, "You want to dance?"

His hands circled her waist. Check. His head lowered. Check. He pulled her closer. Double check.

Her knee flew up aiming for a vulnerable target. At the last moment she pulled to the right meaning to hit him in the thigh instead, only he was already countering her move. Instead of blocking her, their weight went in the same direction, taking them both down.

Jethro tried to catch her, to save her the brunt of his weight. His effort kept her from landing hard. The plush carpeting helped. But then his body slammed down on top of her, and she lost all the air from her lungs.

CHAPTER ELEVEN

LEXI GASPED, BUT no air went in. Unable to breathe, she grabbed at Jethro.

He pushed up on his arms, starring down at her. "It's okay. Stay calm. You've had the air knocked out of you."

She knew that, wanted it back. Every instinct screamed breathe in. But she could only gasp, the breath sticking at the back of her throat. This happened to dancers all the time. She knew what to do but couldn't think.

She was going to die choking on her own air.

"You're okay—" Jethro brushed the hair off her forehead "—it takes a minute. Breathe out first then you'll be able to breathe in."

It went against every action her brain was sending her way, but she was desperate so she followed his instructions and pushed air out. Immediately air flowed back in. She drew in deep breaths. She just may live after all.

The tension went out of him and his body settled on hers again. He laid his forehead on hers. "You scared me."

"I scared me."

"Is that how you fight zombies?"

"No, that's how I fight sloppy drunks except I hit my target. I was trying to save you."

"Thank you."

"You didn't fall for my act." She cringed at the pout in her voice.

"Oh, I enjoyed the performance. I just didn't let it distract me from your purpose."

"Your enemy's goal," she muttered.

He reared back. "You know *The Art of War*?"

The action ground his hips against hers, providing proof his equipment survived the altercation just fine.

She found herself gasping for air again. "There was a copy in my room." The man probably had the book memorized.

"Are you looking to use my library against me, Lexi?"

She noticed he hadn't moved. Why wasn't he moving?

Why wasn't she pushing him away?

"I don't want to be at war with you."

"What do you want?" He finally rolled to the side. He leaned on his elbow and gazed down at her. "Why do you really want to learn to fight?"

She sighed and stared at the ceiling. "I told you, I detest having a babysitter when I go out of the hotel."

"I remember. It makes you feel like a delinquent teenager." He ran his fingers through her hair. "Bad memories?"

"I know you have a file on me," she challenged him. "It probably says I had a privileged upbringing. I did."

"The outside picture doesn't always show all the facts."

She met his dark gaze, trying to read what he felt. "I suppose someone who went through the foster system would know that better than most."

"Privileged doesn't mean happy. You mentioned your life changed when your father died."

"Yes. He was a genius, but he knew how to have fun. Mother wasn't so bad back then. He was a professor and he and my mom homeschooled me. He made learning interesting and he'd take me to class with him sometimes."

"What did he teach?"

"Math. I was twelve when he had an incapacitating stroke. Mother couldn't handle it. She hired someone to care for him and focused all her attention on me. I spent as much time with him as I could. He died when I was fifteen. I'd just graduated from high school. My mother immediately enrolled me at the university. Because of my dad's connections, I was able to do most of my work at home and email in my assignments. Except for piano. I got to go to class for that."

"It sounds like you led a sheltered life."

"It didn't feel like it until it was just mom and me. She loved my dad. He and music were her whole life. When she lost him, first to the stroke and then for good, she focused on the music and I was part of that. She wanted more, bigger, better for me." Lexi picked at the material over her knee. "At first I welcomed the attention. I was missing my dad and the music was something we could share. Until it became clear that what I wanted seemed to matter less and less."

"You wanted to dance."

"Yes! I loved making music, but for me it's more about feeling it. The beat and rhythm connect with something in me and my world comes alive. Mom couldn't—wouldn't—understand that. She saw dance as an unnecessary distraction."

"You got your doctorate at the age of twenty-two." His comment confirmed he'd read the reports given to him.

"A slacker by genius standards. I had to work to support myself the last few years."

"Because you left home when you turned eighteen."

"I couldn't stay any longer. I felt smothered in that house. She was the only family I had so I kept hoping she'd see reason. But the more I pushed for freedom to do things I liked, the tighter she got on the reins, until I felt like a prisoner in my own home." She reached up and pulled the band from her hair, sighed at the release of tension.

"For her it was always about playing, about the performance. Not for me. I had a hard time with the symphony because the conductor's version of the music jarred with what I felt. I played it, but it always felt off to me. That's not the career I wanted."

"And not what your mother wanted to hear."

Red strands of hair fell in her face when she shook her

head. "No. And as long as I was in her house, I had to do things her way." She lifted one shoulder, let it fall. "So I left." She met Jethro's dark gaze. "I had to dance. More than the hidden moments I stole for myself. I longed to learn, to know what my body could do. When she did allow me to go somewhere, it was only with an approved companion. As if I couldn't be trusted out of her sight."

A low growl sounded in the back of his throat. "You know my escorts are there for your safety."

"Yeah, that's what my mother said too. They were just there in the event something happened I wouldn't be alone. It all boils down to a lack of faith in me."

"Lexi, that's not true."

She shrugged. "It's what it feels like."

He swept her hair behind her ear. "How'd you manage on your own?"

"I had a small trust fund my father left me. I rented a room from one of the professors and added cosmetology to my curriculum. I can play most instruments so the symphony hired me as a backup artist. That was kind of fun. Between that and a few other pickup jobs, I managed until I got my doctorate. As soon as I finished my last course, I bought a bus ticket to New York and never looked back."

"The Big Apple. You didn't stay there long."

"I couldn't afford to. That is one expensive burg. And you need to be good, I mean seriously good, to dance in New York. I didn't have the chops or experience they wanted."

"You met Alliyah there."

She nodded. "In a dance class. She was the teacher. Now, she was good. I'd watch her and burn with envy. Not because she'd already been in a couple of off-Broadway productions and was working her way up, but because she made it look effortless. She was so beautiful, so graceful. I wanted to be her."

"How did the two of you end up in Las Vegas?"

"We became friends and then roommates. She got the

chance to do a music video with a hip-hop band as the lead dancer. She talked the artist into using me as a background dancer. The choreographer wasn't too pleased, wanted me to pay for my own flight. It was a tough decision, but I'd be getting paid and it would be my first credit. I went for it. Turned out the choreographer liked us, so we got more work and then he offered us spots in the show he was starting for the Monte Carlo. The money was good so we decided to stay."

"And it wasn't long before the student outreached the teacher."

"Never. Alliyah was a headliner well before me and would have continued to be, except she got pregnant. Jazi was the most important part of her life. She dropped back into the chorus because it was less demanding and allowed her more time with her child."

"If the money was good, why was she moonlighting?"

A sense of aggravated fondness lifted the corners of Lexi's mouth. "Alliyah liked to shop. For herself, for others. Her lack of discipline in that area was the only thing we ever fought over. She had no real money sense. More than once I had to cover the rent because we all had new pretties."

"I'm sorry."

Lexi shook it off. "I didn't mind. We were a family. I just wanted her to be more responsible with her money. For Jazi's sake."

"You cared."

"Well, yeah. Of course. She was my best friend. And I loved Jazi from the moment she was born."

"It shows." He ran his fingers over the back of her hand. "Thank you for everything you've done for her. Knowing you'll be her mother is the only thing that keeps me sane about this whole arrangement."

A wash of emotion flooded her, relief, gratitude, affection and so much more. She turned her hand over and curled her fingers with his. "That's the nicest thing anyone has ever said to me."

"I mean it."

"I know—that's what makes it matter. Goodness." She swiped at the tears leaking out of the corners of her eyes. "I'm a mess." She waved toward him. "I've spilled my guts and now you know my whole life story. What about you? How did you end up in foster care?"

"My mother threw me in the garbage when I was a few weeks old."

Something, maybe the way he looked away, kept her from laughing at his comment. Because surely he couldn't be serious. People didn't throw infants away as if they were trash.

Except sometimes they did.

"I'm so sorry. Did they find her? Did you ever get to know her?"

"No."

That was it; he offered nothing more.

His stiff posture shouted his discomfort. Knowing how reticent he was she imagined he rarely, if ever, spoke of this. She'd always wondered what put him off having a family. He was such a strong, intelligent, competent man. Sure he was overprotective and autocratic at times, but he could also be kind and gentle. No one would ever look at him and see a lost little boy.

This was at the heart of the vulnerability she occasionally glimpsed. Why he allowed so few people to get close.

So why spill his guts now? Why to her?

Duh! Because in spite of his desire to remain autonomous, he was a father and he was struggling to find his way.

Her heart bled for him, but she didn't know how to help him. What she did know was keeping it bottled up solved nothing.

"How do you know it was your mom?"

He went still and a scowl darkened his features. "Who else if not my mother?"

She leaned forward, kept her tone soft, gentle. "Maybe your father, or a grandparent?" Neither were acceptable substitutes, but slightly less traumatic than being rejected by your mother.

How often had she angsted over why her mother didn't love her?

He pulled away from her touch. "Is that supposed to make me feel better—that my whole family threw me away?"

"No." Not letting him push her aside, she wrapped her arms around one of his and propped her chin on his shoulder. "I'm saying you don't know what happened. It takes a lot for a woman to abandon her child."

"Then where was she?" he demanded. "Why didn't she fight for me?"

And there was the little boy.

"Maybe she couldn't. Maybe she died and your dad panicked. Maybe she was a runaway forced to work the streets and her pimp threw you away. Or maybe someone from another town stole you and then couldn't live with what they did so they left you somewhere on the way home."

A heavy sigh lifted his chest. "Oh, that's nice."

"I'm sorry, but an infant in the garbage is ugly. What led to it is going to be just as ugly. Maybe whoever threw you away thought you were dead."

"You're just full of colorful scenarios. Maybe it was a zombie."

"Ha-ha. Haven't you ever made up stories imagining what happened?"

He shook his head. "Being thrown in the trash seemed a pretty clear message to me."

"Not to me. How about this? High school sweethearts very much in love. She gets pregnant at sixteen. He stands by her, but her parents kick her out of the house. It still happens. His parents refuse to take her in so the young couple leaves for the big city. He'll get a job, they'll get an apartment, everything will be fine. Instead they end up on the streets. They have no money, no insurance. You come early. Your dad tries to get your mom to a hospital, but you come too fast. He has to deliver you himself, and then your mom hemorrhages, and he can't stop it.

"Someone finally comes to help him. They call 911. She's dead and you're crying. He's seventeen and afraid. All he can think is if the authorities come they'll take you away. He grabs you and runs. But he has no resources, no way to feed or clothe you. He tries his best, even robs a convenience store, but those supplies don't last long, and it's cold, and you're sickly."

Into the story, Lexi cleared a lump from her throat. Jethro sat still as a stone next to her.

"He wants to take you home except he can't. It was because of his parents and hers that she was gone. He can't go back to that life, to the people who saw honor in death over morals. He needs more supplies so he hides you in a trash can a safe distance away and attempts to rob another store. This time the owner has a shotgun under the counter and your dad is shot and killed. Sometime later you're found in the trash can but the two incidents are never linked."

Silence followed the end of her story. Lexi bit her lip, waiting for Jethro's response, which remained unvoiced for long minutes.

"You do realize," he finally said, "in this version I'm responsible for the destruction of my parents."

"Oh, come on." Frustrated with his pessimism, she reared back and socked him in the arm. "Clearly this was a story of two people who loved their son so much they'd give anything for him, including their lives."

He hooked an arm around her waist and pulled her into his lap. He lifted her chin on the edge of his hand. "What makes you such an optimist?"

"Choice." She gave the easy answer. Then, because the moment called for honesty, she sighed and admitted, "And maybe a touch of defiance. At home it was a form of rebellion and when I left home I wasn't going to let my mother's predictions of failure pull me down. Optimism was my only option. I chose to believe in myself. I chose to believe everything was going to work out. And mostly it does."

His dark eyes roved over her face. "I wish it were that simple."

She cupped his cheek. "It can be that simple. Stop letting the past rob you of a future. Create a story you can live with and make it your reality. You're an amazing man, Jethro. Choose to look to the future with hope."

"I'm too old to change now."

She shook her finger in his face. "You wouldn't say that if we were talking about a business deal."

"Business is different."

"Why?"

"Business doesn't involve emotions."

She laughed, letting him lead the conversation away from his past. "How can you be so successful and believe that malarkey? Business is totally ruled by emotions."

"Business is based on facts and numbers."

"Yes, and once you have the facts and numbers, what guides the decision? Emotion. If you want to call it your gut or instinct, go ahead, but bottom line it's all about how those facts and figures make you feel that shifts the balance when it comes time to make the decision."

He ground his teeth together. "Has anyone ever told you you're a pest?"

"No." She postured and patted the hair at the back of her neck. "I'm perfect."

"Really?" His fingers threaded through her hair and he drew her to him. "Let me taste to be sure."

His mouth claimed hers, his tongue surging inward to tangle with hers. He tasted of man and mocha. And he smelled fabulous. She wrapped her arms around his neck and let sensation carry her away.

Jethro shifted, tilting Lexi's head to deepen the kiss. She was no longer in his arms but sprawled on the floor with him above her. She savored his weight, his warmth, his strength. Pulling him closer, she held on tight, afraid he'd come to his senses. She'd waited for this, wanted this for so long. Since the night he broke into her apartment and demanded the truth.

Her head binged a warning, but her heart sang and her body soared so she let reason go fly.

She panted, his talented fingers and hungry lips driving her into a frenzy of need. Always so cool, so controlled, but not now, not here. He divested them of their clothes in mere seconds. Then his hands were everywhere stroking, caressing. And squeezing. Exquisite.

Who knew?

She tried to reciprocate, longing to taste him, to explore the hard body pressed to hers, but all she could do was cling to him as he played her body like a fine instrument. Smoothing fingers over slick skin, she dragged heavy lids up to see him. Her whole body clenched to find all his brooding intensity focused on her. His eyes darkened to a blue deeper than midnight and blazed with the heat of passion. His features were drawn tight with the primitive drive to claim the woman in his arms.

"So beautiful." He trailed a finger along her jaw, down her neck and lower. "So soft, yet I feel the strength in you. So sexy." He lowered his head and his tongue followed the path of his finger.

Lexi shivered, thrilled to be the target of his intense regard. The look in those dark eyes cherished her, telling her he was with her mind, body, and spirit, that he hungered for her above all others. Touch reinforced the message, building anticipation, heightening the senses, seducing her when there was no need for seduction.

"Jethro." Beyond thought, she arched her dancer's body into his hold, offering him everything. And he caught her, lifting her to the heights until he roared his satisfaction. And she shattered in his arms.

CHAPTER TWELVE

SPRAWLED HALF ON Jethro and half on the lush white carpeting, Lexi had barely caught her breath when a scream echoed down the hall and from the baby monitor. And then another, and another.

She went from boneless satisfaction to alert mother in a blink.

"Oh, no." Despair rolled through Lexi. "Jazi."

She hopped to her feet, realized she was naked and looked frantically for her clothes. The few items she'd worn were scattered all over the room. As another scream sounded, she gave up looking and grabbed Jethro's shirt, pulling it on as she raced down the hall.

Jethro yanked on his dress pants and followed on her heels.

She'd prayed Jazi had outgrown her screaming fits. The lack of them over the last few weeks had made Lexi hopeful they were a thing of the past.

She reached the bedroom, her heart shredding at the sight of Jazi sitting straight up in the middle of the bed, body rigid, tears streaming down her face, shrill screams pouring from her throat.

Lexi wrapped the baby in her arms and rocked her. "It's okay, Jazi, you're safe. I'm here. I've got you."

The little girl hung limp in her arms; the screams continued. It was like she didn't even hear Lexi. Still she held the little girl and rocked her, talking softly to her.

Jethro paced next to the bed.

"What's wrong? What set her off?"

"I don't know. Maybe a dream. She was cranky when I put her to bed. Maybe my screams disturbed her earlier and she woke up scared."

Lexi hummed softly for a few minutes and Jazi stopped screaming. She panted, drawing in deep breaths. And then she started screaming again.

Her distress broke Lexi's heart. Jazi was so tiny, so fragile and nothing Lexi did helped. She felt helpless and near to tears herself. Worse, Jethro was a witness to all of it.

"You should call Clay—" she cleared her throat, forcing the words past the lump sitting there "—and assure him she's okay in case someone complains."

"No one is going to complain." Jethro ran a hand over her head. "The penthouse suites are built to withstand wild parties. They're pretty much soundproof."

Rocking Jazi, she swallowed hard. "Thank you."

"Let me try." He held out his arms.

Lexi tightened her arms around Jazi, hating to give her up, but the need to ease her distress was stronger, so she lifted her up and Jethro gathered her into his arms. He laid her head against his shoulder and placed a hand in the small of her back.

"Breathe with me, Jazi." His chest rose and fell, Jazi moving with each breath. He breathed deep and steady, talking to her until she started breathing along with him. Slowly she calmed and the screams lessened and then stopped. Jazi snuggled against his bare chest, seeming to take comfort in his warmth.

Her breath hitched a few times but she appeared to be past the storm.

Lexi let out a breath she hadn't known she was holding. Thank goodness.

Jazi held out her hand to Lexi. Love welling up, she leapt up to take her, but Jazi had other ideas. She wanted Lexi, but she wasn't letting go of Jethro. He solved the problem by pulling her close with Jazi between them.

Lexi wrapped her arms around his waist, letting the tension slip away. These fits of Jazi's were so hard on the little girl. They were tough on Lexi too. It tore her up to see the toddler so upset. But this time she hadn't been alone. She'd had help.

She laid her head on Jethro's shoulder and leaned on him, an indulgence she rarely allowed. Soaking in his warmth, like Jazi took comfort in his nearness, in his company. She felt as close to him in this moment as she had in the throes of passion.

It occurred to her that parenting with a partner might have some merit to it. Dangerous thoughts, because something happened to her while she watched him soothe Jazi. Something that changed everything for Lexi. She'd fallen in love with Jethro Calder.

That night the three of them ended up in Jethro's big bed. She fell asleep wrapped in his arms and dreamt of them becoming a real family. Jethro smiled more, Jazi thrived under her father's devoted attention and Lexi found the perfect balance between commitment and independence.

In the dream they were walking through a house with a white picket fence in a pretty neighborhood. Jazi exclaimed over a room with a pink canopy bed, an aquarium, bookshelves full of books and an artist easel. She ran inside and began to play. Farther along there was an office for Jethro and in the back a long room had a dance floor and mirrors on one end and a piano and assorted instruments on the other. Lexi wanted to explore but Jethro pulled her down to the master bedroom, a beautiful retreat she couldn't remember because dreamy Jethro tugged her into his arms and the dream took an erotic turn.

Contentment lured her into sleeping longer than usual and she woke to find Jethro gone. She lay there curled around Jazi wishing he'd woken her, wishing they could have talked.

Waking up in Jethro's bed gave her the perfect opportunity to indulge herself in his grotto shower. Water rained down on her, hot and steamy. She stood on smooth rocks while green fronds draped over the top and sides of the glass partition.

But the luxury failed to distract her from her dream. It didn't take a massive IQ to see what her subconscious was telling her. She'd fallen for the hard-headed Jethro so now her heart wanted the daddy-makes-three mix with a flip side of picket fences and rose gardens.

That so wasn't her.

She hadn't had a lot of relationships. She liked to keep things light and loose. Fun while it lasted and friends down the road. No baggage, no obligations. No one telling her what to do. Just being with each other while it felt right.

And that was the problem. The dream had felt right. She'd woken up happy. And she couldn't shake the desire to know that feeling every day. She lifted her face to the rainfall spray and wondered how that was possible when Jethro came with a load of baggage, untold obligations and a fine-tuned art of telling people what to do.

But he'd also given her free reign in the kitchen, which allowed her a sense of comfort in a strange home. He'd found her a place to dance, which was necessary to her well-being. And he'd encouraged her to work with Veronica, an opportunity she'd never have had if he hadn't introduced them.

He got her like no one else ever had.

How did she walk away from that?

Lexi canceled her morning meeting with Veronica to spend extra time with Jazi to make sure she felt secure and suffered no lingering upset from the night before, but the little tyrant demanded to go to "school," as Jazi called the nursery.

Relieved to see Jazi being her usual spirited self, Lexi

took her down to the nursery. She swung by Veronica's office but the door was locked and it was obvious she was out. Lexi returned to the penthouse where she spent the morning brooding.

Last night had been in turns earth-shattering, devastating and sublime.

She'd give anything to know what he was thinking today. So of course she'd texted him.

Twice.

Still no answer.

What she really wished was to go back to the time before Jazi had started screaming. How would it have played out? Never had she been more open with a man, physically or emotionally. And there wasn't a doubt in her mind it was the same for him.

Had the intimacy been too much for him? Is that why he hadn't answered her text or called?

He'd been so patient with Jazi last night, so gentle in the face of her hysteria. It had been him, not Lexi to soothe Jazi. Lexi did not look forward to dealing with those episodes on her own.

And so ended one loop as another began.

No more.

Needing a distraction she decided to make herself lunch. She'd just started putting together a sandwich when a knock came at the penthouse door. She opened it to find a tall dark-haired man standing before her.

"Lexi."

"Ryan."

Handsome in an exotic way, she recognized him from the charity event. If Jethro and his foster brothers ever lost their fortunes, they could take up modeling and get it all back.

"Can I come in for a moment?"

"Sure." She stepped aside, curious as to what had caused Pinnacle's general counsel to seek her out. Before she moved in, Jethro had mentioned a contract, but that was nearly a month ago. Was this his response to last night's intimacy? His way of telling her nothing had changed? "Will Jethro be joining us?"

"No. Something came up in New York and as our offices are closed all week for Thanksgiving, he's handling it."

Right. Jethro had mentioned the office would be closed. "But you're working?"

He shrugged. "I'm happiest when I'm working. I'm a lot like Jethro in that way. Or how he used to be."

Used to be? Lexi latched on to the phrase. Did that mean Jethro had changed in some way?

"Be thankful Jethro is occupied—he's in a foul mood today."

News to her. Since she hadn't heard from him, even though she'd texted him.

"I'm making lunch." She led Ryan to the kitchen where sandwich makings were spread over the counter. "Would you like a ham and provolone on wheat?"

"Actually, that does sound good." He slid onto a stool at the counter across from her and set a folder on the granite countertop.

She waved at the condiments and veggies in front of her. "What do you want on it?"

He surveyed the options. "No tomato."

"Coming up." She added lettuce, pickles and mustard to the ham, cheese and mayo, cut the sandwich in half, plated it with a pickle spear and handed it to him. After she passed him a napkin, she started on a second one for herself.

"Thank you. I can't remember the last time someone made me a sandwich." He took a bite and nodded. "It's good."

She licked mustard from her thumb. "What can I do for you?"

He wiped his mouth. "Nothing. I have something for you." Ryan reached for the folder and pulled out some papers.

"The contract about Jazi." Lexi's heart skipped a beat. "Jethro told me he'd want one."

"No, Jethro is still making changes to that contract. Ask him about it would you? Then we may get somewhere." There was a sardonic tone to the comment that suggested the men were at odds over the issue. "This is something totally different. This is for your contribution to Jack Rabbits song."

She eyed him, ignoring the pages he shoved toward her, wondering instead about what changes Jethro could be making to the adoption contract that had Ryan concerned.

"The band asked me to thank you again for your help. They really enjoyed working with you."

Lexi blinked at him, not following until she recalled he'd mentioned the band Jack Rabbits. "Oh, yeah." Remembering the jam session, she smiled. "It was fun."

He nodded at the papers. "And profitable."

"What do you mean?" She reached for the pile of papers. On top was a sizable check with her name on it. "I don't understand. What's this for?"

"It's a consultant fee for your contribution to the song. Your name will be in the credits and you'll also get royalties from the sales."

Weak-kneed she walked around to sit next to him at the counter. "This is crazy. I didn't do anything. I mean it was just a few simple comments at an informal gathering. I didn't expect anything from it."

"Jethro is big on people getting the proper credit. He called me that night and gave me the terms. All you have to do is sign the contract and the check is yours."

"Terms?"

He finished chewing his last bite before answering. "You should read it before signing, but he negotiated well for you. It's better than standard. And the band was happy to sign, said they'd like to work with you again sometime. They're positive it's going to be a winner."

She stared at the check. "I don't know what to say."

"No need to say anything." He reached across to set his plate in the sink. "Let me know if you have any questions, otherwise sign both copies, keep one and I'll give you the check when you drop the other off at my office."

"Thank you. You didn't need to go out of your way to bring it to me. I could have come to your office."

He shrugged. "It's what I do." His gaze roamed over the open space. "And truthfully, I was hoping to meet Jasmine."

Of course. He was curious about Jethro's daughter. "Sorry, she's down in the nursery. Craft time is her favorite part of the day."

He stared at her for a moment, giving her the impression he wanted to say something. But he thought better of it. He simply nodded. "Happy Thanksgiving."

And he left.

Lexi stared at the papers in her hands. So many emotions roiled through her veering wildly from love to fear and everything in between. She'd spent the whole morning brooding, her mind running one vicious loop after another. Worrying about her and Jethro. Worrying about her and Jazi. Worrying about the past. Wondering about the future.

Papers in hand she returned to the kitchen and her abandoned sandwich. She carried the plate along with the papers to the table and sat. While she ate, she read. For a contract it was fairly straightforward. Her simple suggestions earned her royalties in the song, a partial amount to be paid up front; the rest to be paid quarterly. She felt like a fraud accepting the money. She'd just been happy to be included in the jam session, wouldn't even have spoken up if not for Jethro.

Still, she signed the contract, considered it as a down payment on a house. No more apartments for her and Jazi.

She'd never expected he'd push a contract on the band.

Why had he? Ryan said Jethro had a thing about people getting credit for their work, but the situation had been so informal she'd had no expectation of receiving any credit. Plus the band sang for Pinnacle's label. It seemed odd he'd put her welfare above the band's.

Unless he cared for her.

Which brought her back to the one question she kept shying away from. Did they have a future together? Could her dream become a reality?

A month ago she would have panicked at the thought of giving up her independence. Taking on Jazi didn't count because Lexi remained in control. She got to make all their life decisions. At least until Jazi got older. Allowing a man into the mix was a whole different matter. Especially one who was overly protective and used to taking charge.

Now she panicked at the thought of leaving.

She wondered if he still felt the same way about not having a family now that he knew what it felt like to have one.

Did no response mean he didn't want to talk or was he just busy?

Lexi chewed her lower lip, torn between the need to know what last night meant to him and proceeding cautiously. The last thing she wanted was to make Jethro second-guess his agreement to let her have Jazi. If she suggested mutual custody, he might take it as an opportunity to take back full custody. And then she'd lose both of them.

Ryan's mention of Thanksgiving prompted the realization that the holiday was only a few days away. Traditionally people spent the day with friends or family or both. She and Alliyah always made a point of inviting other dancers also away from their families.

Would Jethro spend the day with his family or with her and Jazi?

She rubbed her shirt right over her heart, surprised by how important the question was.

It would be nice if they could all celebrate the day together. His foster brothers were curious about Jazi. Jackson stopped by one day on the pretext of looking for Jethro.

He actually got to see Jazi, though she'd been down for her nap. And now Ryan had found a reason to come to the penthouse. And of course Clay had become one of Jazi's favorite people.

They were Jethro's brothers and after hearing his story, she knew what that meant. Lexi longed to get to know them better. And for them to get to know Jazi.

But Jethro had looked grim when she'd mentioned Jackson's visit, and he'd made it clear he preferred to keep the two sides of his family separate. Lexi understood he was trying to save heartache for all concerned.

Maybe that was the answer to her dilemma. If he asked her to join him and his friends for Thanksgiving, she'd know he was open to a relationship.

Jethro tapped his pen against his desk. Rage roiled under the surface of his calm facade. Fury at himself for allowing temptation to win over his will, an unwanted distraction when he needed to be at his sharpest.

Luckily he had Jackson's assistant, Sierra, to help him throughout the day. A Harvard attorney, she made the Fabulous Four look good. She lived in the hotel and had been the one to take the call from the New York office.

He wasn't purposely dodging Lexi's texts. He needed his focus to deal with the distribution issue in New York. Pinnacle had a new game releasing on Thanksgiving. They'd chosen the date to maximize sales on Black Friday. The problem with their distribution center had the power to negate those sales if he didn't resolve it in the next two days.

After his third two-hour call, he could no longer deny the need to fly to New York. Part of him experienced relief at having a reason to get away for a few days. It would give him time to think about what had happened and what he wanted to do. The other half of him hated to lose even a moment of his time with Lexi and Jazi.

Waking up with Lexi in his arms rated as the sweetest

moment of his life except now he'd have the taste of her in his head for the rest of his life.

He'd wanted her from the minute she'd walked up to the bar in The Beacon. Setting up house with her under those circumstances boardered on insanity. He might fool others with the excuse that he needed to be sure Jazi would be safe, but he knew the truth. He'd been indulging himself, pretending he was part of something special, the family he'd never have.

He didn't deserve it, but he'd wanted the time with his daughter. And Lexi.

He'd known from the beginning he'd need to control himself. To keep it in his pants.

So much for his famed self-discipline.

"I'll make our flight arrangements. Jet or commercial?" Sierra closed her portfolio.

"Jet." He hated to pull the pilot and crew from their vacations, but they were paid to be on call and the situation warranted it. "There's no need for you to go and ruin your time off."

"It's okay," she assured him. "I'll visit family."

Something in her tone brought his attention around to her. "Everything okay? You don't sound too enthusiastic."

She sighed. "It's complicated. I wasn't going to go this year, but this seems to be a sign I should."

"You don't believe in signs."

She gave a half laugh. "Not usually, no." Then she changed the subject. "Should I leave the return date open?"

"No. Whatever happens with distribution, good or bad, we'll be back for Thanksgiving."

"Works for me." Her fingers flew over her phone as she texted the pilot. "I've been looking forward to a traditional turkey dinner at Jackson and Grace's new house."

"Yeah." The couple had invited the group, including Lexi and Jazi, to join them for the holiday.

Jethro had yet to make up his mind on whether he'd attend or spend the day at home. He'd like nothing better than to bring Lexi and his daughter with him to the celebration, but he couldn't—wouldn't—do that to himself or his friends. Once Jazi left his life, every future Thanksgiving would be haunted by the memory of the one holiday he got to spend with his daughter.

Sierra's phone pinged and she announced, "Wheels up in an hour. Meet you downstairs in thirty minutes?"

Didn't leave much time to pack and say goodbye. "Perfect."

Rocked by Jethro's news, Lexi followed him down the hall. "Thirty minutes isn't long to pack. You should have called me." She turned into her room, her mind already occupied with what to take.

"You're not going." Jethro stood in her doorway.

She swung to face him. "I thought you wanted Jazi and me to travel with you."

"Not this time. There's no point. I'll be tied up in meetings until this is resolved." His features were set in hard lines.

"Oh." She should be relieved. Instead she fretted at the timing of his absence.

He headed for his room. She followed, watched as he pulled down a suitcase in his closet.

"I was hoping we could talk."

"We will." He assured her. "When I get back."

She crossed her arms over her chest. Why wasn't she reassured by his promise? "How long will you be gone?"

"I'll be back for Thanksgiving." He packed quickly and methodically.

Some of her tension eased. At least he wasn't skipping out on the holiday. "Good. What are we going to do? Shall I plan to cook?"

"I'll let you know." He zipped his bag and set it on its wheels. And then he was in front of her.

She placed a hand on his heart. He was dressed in jeans and a lightweight black sweater. "You're leaving already?"

"I want to stop by the nursery and say goodbye to Jazi." He cupped her cheek. "Will you miss me?"

"Maybe. Probably." She lowered her eyes. "A lot." His lips caressed her forehead. "Will you think of me?"

He made a sound low in his throat. "Too much." Lifting her chin on the edge of his hand, he claimed her mouth in a long, hard kiss. "I'll call you." And then he was gone.

Weak-kneed, she dropped to the floor and buried her face in her hands. As far as goodbyes went, it left her breathless. If only it didn't feel so final.

Ten minutes later a knock sounded at the door. Lexi swiped at her cheeks and climbed to her feet.

She opened the door to Velveth and a totally distraught Jazi. The woman gave Lexi an apologetic look as she cradled Jazi to her slim chest. "Mr. Calder wanted to bring her up, but I convinced him it was better not to prolong the farewell."

"Of course." Guilt slammed into Lexi. Some mother she was, moping in self-pity when her daughter was suffering. She should have considered how upset Jazi would get hearing another goodbye when she'd already lost her mother, Lexi, and Diana and family. She was too young to understand the difference between a temporary parting and a permanent one.

And Lexi was old enough to know it was just a matter of time.

"Mama!" Jazi reacted to the sound of Lexi's voice by launching herself out of Velveth's arms and into Lexi's. Little arms wrapped around her neck while sobs racked her tiny frame. "Daddy, bye-bye!"

The words stopped Lexi cold. Her heart clenched. First because it thrilled her to be called Mama. It implied a long-term acceptance that validated the connection between them. But her use of Daddy concerned Lexi for the same reason. Especially under the circumstances.

She cleared her throat. "I know baby, he'll be back."

Jazi just cried harder.

Sympathy stamped the nursery manager's soft features. "Mr. Calder looked as devastated as she is when he left. He's quite devoted. He comes to watch her play every day."

"Every day?"

Velveth nodded, her short black hair flowing to and fro with the gesture. The nursery manager placed her hand softly on Jazi's back for a moment and then turned and left.

Lexi cuddled her daughter close and turned into the apartment. She carried her to her room, climbed into bed with her and pulled the throw over them. She hummed softly, determined to be strong for her daughter.

CHAPTER THIRTEEN

Two days went by. Lexi sat in Jazi's room with the fish book in her lap. She watched Jazi play and brooded about not hearing from Jethro beyond exchanging a few texts.

She supposed she should be happy he was making headway with the distributors, but she'd prefer to know what he planned for Thanksgiving.

Giving up on getting a direct answer from him, she'd decided earlier that she and Jazi deserved a turkey dinner regardless if Jethro joined them or not, so she'd made up a shopping list and sent it to Brennan. She couldn't dredge up the enthusiasm to shop when she knew she'd spend the whole trip pouting or brooding. Or hounding Clay for details of the Fabulous Four's holiday plans.

She'd save herself that humiliation thank you very much.

She looked up to see Jazi had dragged a stool over to the dresser and she held the fish food in her hand.

"No, pumpkin, we already fed Fishy."

"More."

"More will make him sick." Lexi took the fish food away. She tapped the bowl. "Say, *Hi, Fishy.*"

"Hi, Fishy." Jazi hopped down, ran out of the room. She came back a moment later with Lexi's phone. "Mama." She handed the phone to Lexi. "Daddy. Say hi."

Lexi closed her eyes briefly. She was still calling Jethro Daddy. Nothing Lexi said dissuaded her. In fact, if Lexi pushed too hard, Jazi went into another weeping fit.

"He'll be home tomorrow." She set the phone down on the book.

"Tomorrow?" the girl parroted as if she knew what it meant.

"Yes, after you go to sleep and then wake up, he'll be home." But would it be to stay?

These past few days had convinced Lexi of the need for a change. She loved Jethro and the more she contemplated their time together, the more she believed he'd changed. He hadn't wanted a family. Because of his past, he believed he wasn't worthy of one.

"Daddy!" Jazi insisted, pushing the phone toward Lexi.

He couldn't be more wrong. As his daughter's demand illustrated.

He may be stoic in nature and protective of his privacy, but he'd put Jazi's needs first over and over. And he'd done everything possible to make Lexi feel welcome and comfortable.

She'd never felt more cherished in a man's arms. There was a difference between making out and making love. And she'd been well loved. Both raw and elemental, the connection between them burned so deep it touched her soul forever imprinting his essence within her.

"Okay." She picked up the phone and hit the speed dial for Jethro. Expecting it to go to voice mail the same as the other times she called, she put it on speaker for Jazi to hear. "But Jethro's very busy, baby. He may not be able to talk to us."

Uncaring of the warning, Jazi climbed into her lap as the phone rang.

"Hey," his deep voice came on the line. "I'm headed into another meeting so I only have a couple of minutes. It looks like we'll have to burn the midnight oil to get this resolved. I may not be back until Thanksgiving."

"Daddy!" Jazi grabbed the phone. "Hi!"

A brief moment of silence followed.

Lexi wished she could have warned him. "Someone has been missing you. She insisted we call to say hi."

"Hey, Jazi." The words were gravel rough. A rumbling sounded on the other end, perhaps the clearing of his throat. His voice was clearer when he continued. "I miss you too."

Encouraged, Jazi chattered on. Her vocabulary suffered under her enthusiasm, so only a few words made sense. But Jethro engaged her with questions and she rattled out answers until he indicated it was time for him to go.

Her response was more than clear. "Love you."

"Baby." The gravel was back. "I miss you both. I... I'll see you soon."

Lexi woke on Thanksgiving to a sunny day in Las Vegas. Sliding into her robe she went down the hall to see if Jethro made it home. She gave his door a brief knock and opened it. The room was empty.

Disappointed, she checked her phone. There was a text from him advising his flight was delayed due to storms in New York.

She checked the weather in New York and found forecasts for thunderstorms for the whole day. She hoped he somehow found a way out. Jazi would be very disappointed if he didn't make it home.

Who was she fooling? *She'd* be disappointed if he didn't make it home.

She hopped into the shower and then dressed. She peeked in on Jazi and decided to let her sleep. Over her first cup of coffee, Lexi saw she'd missed a call from Jethro. He'd left a voice mail that was garbled and a bit broken up.

"We just got appr...for liftoff. Wanted to talk...you... but...can't wait...storms. Clay will...going... Jackson's... bye."

Okay, that was as clear as jelly beans. She played it again and learned nothing more. The call came in a little before nine and the flight was about three hours, plus an hour to get home from the landing site, which would put him home around one.

But was he coming here or going to Jackson's?

And what was Clay doing?

She knew no more now than she had before. Back to waiting.

She sipped her coffee and tried not to let it get to her. Tried not to worry that he preferred to spend the day with his friends than with her and Jazi. Tried to pretend everything was fine. Tried and failed. Add frustration to worry, longing, hope.

She could call Clay, but she imagined how pathetic she'd sound and decided against that conversation.

So she got busy instead. She pulled out apples, sugar and flour and began paring. She'd start dinner by making dessert. The apple pie sat cooling on the counter when she heard Jazi stirring.

Lexi got her up and dressed while fending off questions of when Daddy would be home.

"He's on his way but it takes a long time to fly from New York to here."

"Long time?"

"Yes. Hours and hours." How did you explain time to a two-year-old? "He'll be here later."

"Later? Daddy come later?"

"Yep, later. Are you hungry?"

She looked so sad, Lexi lifted her up and pretended to eat her tummy. The childish giggles soothed her own sadness.

"I'm hungry." She ate some more tummy.

"Stop!" Jazi tried to push her shirt down so Lexi couldn't get to her belly. "I hungry."

"You're hungry?" She met Jazi's laughing blue gaze. "Do you want tummy for breakfast or pancakes?"

"Pancakes." Jazi clapped her hands.

Happy she'd distracted the child, Lexi carried her to the kitchen. "Mama wants pancakes too."

* * *

A little before eleven a knock sounded at the door.

"Daddy!" Jazi raced to get there before Lexi.

"No, baby. Daddy will come later."

She glanced through the peephole, warned herself not to get her hopes up and opened the door to Clay. "Hi."

"Clay!" Jazi wrapped herself around his leg.

He looked down at her and then up at Lexi obviously bemused by the show of affection.

She shrugged. "She likes you."

"She does?"

"Oh, yeah. She thinks you're funny."

His brow wrinkled as his bemusement increased. "All I do is drive you."

She lifted a brow. "Have you heard yourself when you drive? Plus, you call her jelly bean."

The corner of his mouth lifted in acknowledgment. He swung Jazi up into his arms. "Hey, jelly bean." He carried her inside.

She kissed his cheek. And he flushed.

Lexi smiled and headed into the kitchen. "What can I do for you?"

"I've been instructed to pick you up."

She went still. "And do what with me?"

"Take you to Jackson's. We're having Thanksgiving dinner at his new place."

She swung around. "By Jethro?"

"Grace is cooking."

"You know what I'm asking, Clay." It would be easy to assume Clay was here at Jethro's urging. The garbled message could have meant Clay will pick you up. But she wouldn't be tripped up. This was too important to risk assuming anything. "Was it Jethro who instructed you to pick me up?"

"Everyone agreed. Jazi is family." He set the little girl on her feet and she ran off to the media room. "You deserve to be with the family for Thanksgiving."

Leaning back against the counter, arms crossed over her chest, she demanded, "Everyone but Jethro?"

"You are relentless." He lifted a lid on a steaming pot of carrots.

"I love him, Clay."

"Then fight for him, Lexi." He clipped out the demand.

"I want to." No, that wasn't right. "I'm going to. But this isn't the way."

He propped his hands on his waist. "Why not?"

"Come on." Needing movement, she grabbed a dish towel and wiped up the water the lid had dripped. "You know how he is about Jazi. He hasn't stopped any of you from meeting her, but he hasn't shared her with you either."

"He's a private man. But I've seen the way he looks at you. And he's changed these past few weeks, found an inner calmness. It's good to see him happy. He just needs a nudge."

A nudge? To get through Jethro's thick skull she was going to need a wrecking ball by four. But calm was good, happy even better. She soaked in the words of encouragement. All the more reason to stand her ground.

"It's more than that. He's very protective of all of you. He doesn't want anyone to become attached to her, to be hurt when I take her away."

"You mean he doesn't want us trying to change his mind."

"That may be part of it, yes."

Enough already. Didn't he know how much she longed to go? To spend time with Jethro and the people he held so dear? The fact that he hadn't invited her festered like a raw burn. It didn't help that she knew all the reasons why he hadn't; she wanted to celebrate with him. But only if he wanted her there.

"I just know surprising him with our appearance isn't a good idea."

"Well then, let *us* have some time with her. Come over for an hour. Jethro isn't due until one." He ran a large hand through thick blond hair. "I don't want to put your relationship at risk, but she's essentially our niece and we want to get to know her.

"I'm pretty sure that's what he's trying to prevent."

"We're adults. How much damage can happen in an hour? If Jethro objects, I'll say I shanghaied you."

"Mama." Jazi came running in on bare feet. "More juice."

While Lexi refilled her sippy cup, Jazi tugged on Clay's pant leg. "Daddy?"

Clay shot a questioning glance Lexi's way.

She cringed as she shrugged. "She started in when he left and I can't get her to go back to his name."

Clay hunkered down to talk to Jazi. "He's on his way, jelly bean. He'll be here soon."

"Later?"

He swiped her nose. "Yes. Later."

Jazi looked so sad Lexi sighed and gave in. It felt like they'd been holed up for the last three days, constantly waiting for Jethro's return. Jazi had been so good, but she could really use the distraction.

"Okay, you win. We'll go. But only until twelve thirty. I want to be long gone by the time Jethro gets there."

Though he argued, Lexi insisted on driving her own car. Really there was no need for him to break up his celebration to take her home. As for her required escort, she'd be following him there and she promised to go straight back to the hotel with no stops and no passing go.

Jackson and Grace Black lived in an extravagant trilevel mansion in the hills of Henderson overlooking Las Vegas. The building had a majestic presence with beautiful stone finishes and white columns. A large palm tree shaded the circular drive.

There were no near neighbors. On the way down in the elevator Clay told her Jackson had bought the ten lots surrounding his to ensure his privacy. The only people he'd consider selling to were his foster brothers.

"Do you think you'll build here someday?" she asked Clay as they walked to the door.

"Maybe. We used to joke about having a compound. At least here we'd get to spread out. And I can always travel or buy a second home somewhere else if I feel crowded." He gave a hard knock but didn't wait for the door to be opened. He walked straight in. "I heard Jethro was looking at plans."

Lexi had no time to think about the pang his announcement struck in her heart. People came from all directions to welcome her and Jazi. Or so it seemed. There were actually only the four of them. Clay, Jackson, Ryan and Grace, who came forward and wrapped Lexi and Jazi in a warm hug.

"Welcome to our home. I'm so glad you came. And this is our beautiful Jazi. I'm Aunt Grace."

Jazi peeped up shyly.

"Will you come to me?" Grace held out her arms.

"Grace," her fiancé admonished her.

"Pooh." The slim brunette waved him off. "If I only get an hour, I'm making the most of it."

"Pooh," Jazi echoed and giggled.

"See—" Grace grinned "—she agrees with me." She held her arms out to Jazi. "Won't you come to me? I have treats for you downstairs."

Suddenly shy, Jazi laid her head on Lexi's shoulder.

"It's okay," she whispered, then loud enough for all to hear, "These are Daddy's brothers. You know Clay." She moved so Jazi had a view of Clay, starting with him because she already knew him. "And this is Ryan. Jackson and his fiancée, Grace. Can you say hi?"

"Hi."

TERESA CARPENTER   175

Progress.

Once Lexi finished the intros, she set Jazi on her feet. "Can you take Grace's hand and we'll go see what treats she has?"

Grace held out her hand and Jazi took it, earning a bright smile.

"This way," Grace led them past a lovely cream-and-dove-gray living room and a grand curved staircase to a game room down a short set of stairs. TVs were mounted on every wall. Plenty of large comfortable chairs hugged the walls offering a view of the huge table in the middle of the room currently dressed in the colors of fall and set for a formal dinner.

"Is that a billiard table?"

"It is. I had it custom-made to be converted into a dining table for bigger events. It's tapered on the sides so people can sit at it. I was hoping you would be staying, so I set us up down here."

"I'm sorry you went to extra trouble."

"I'm not. I enjoy a pretty table. And the guys can watch the game." She continued through the large room to a table on the far side with so many cookies, pastries and candies displayed it looked like a bake sale.

"I hope you don't mind—" Grace softly touched Lexi's arm "—but since we missed her birthday and I didn't have time to get a gift, we all have a little something for her."

Jackson stepped into the adjacent media room and came back with a plethora of colorful gift bags.

"Goodness." Lexi was overwhelmed with their generosity. Jazi, she had no doubt, would love it. "That really wasn't necessary."

"We wanted to." Grace called Jazi over. "She's a part of Jethro, a part of us."

Jazi squealed when she saw the packages. She came running and tissue went flying. The first bag, from Clay, contained a colorful book of butterflies. Jazi sat right where she stood and began to flip through the pages.

Lexi glanced at Clay. He beamed and bent to point out Violet the purple butterfly. "Jethro said she liked books."

"I think this will be a new favorite." Lexi climbed down on the floor next to Jazi. "This one is from Ryan."

Jazi dug into the bag and pulled out a toy almost as tall as she was. It was a magnetic drawing set, with a pen attached for drawing. She started to play while Lexi lifted her gaze to Ryan. "Thank you. She's going to love this."

Lexi directed Jazi to the next gift. "From Uncle Jackson."

"Unka Jackson," Jazi repeated.

"That's me, kiddo." Jackson dropped down beside her as she pulled out an eight-inch porcelain cylinder hand painted with pink flowers. Jazi shook it.

"No, sweetie, it's a kaleidoscope. You look in it." He took it and put it to his eye to show her how it worked. Then held it to her eye and turned it.

"Ooh." There was wonder in the childish exclamation. She insisted on showing Lexi.

"It's beautiful." Lexi glanced at Jackson over Jazi's head. "I've never seen one with such pretty colors."

"It's made with real precious gems."

"Jackson! She's two."

"And it may be the only thing she ever gets from me."

She had no answer for him, so she carefully wrapped the extravagant gift. "I'll keep it safe for her."

"It's a toy," he protested. "It's meant to be played with."

"We'll bring it out on special occasions until she gets a little older."

"This is from me." Grace joined them on the floor, leaning against Jackson as she held out a small square box gaily wrapped in red, a tiny white bow propped on top.

"More?" Lexi watched Jazi tear into the pretty paper. "What do you say to everyone, Jazi?"

"Thank you."

The two-year-old showed no delicacy for the packaging and soon held a slim silver bracelet from which five fili-greed hearts dangled. Each heart held a gemstone.

"Pity." Jazi held it right in front of Lexi's face to show her.

"Very pretty." And way too expensive. Just another example of these people's easy wealth. But also of their affection for this child they cared for simply because they loved her father. "Shall we put it on you?"

Jazi held up her wrist. She loved to play dress up. Lexi set the latch and Jazi wiggled her wrist delighted with the flash of the gems.

"They're our birthstones," Grace said, "so she'll always have something to remember us."

Jazi hopped up and threw herself into Grace's arms. "Thank you."

Grace hugged the small body to her, tears shimmering in her eyes. "Please stay."

Jazi wiggled free and went off to play.

Grace's comment was both encouraging and heartbreaking. And required a conversation with Jethro before Lexi could commit.

"What's going on here?" A harsh male voice demanded from across the room.

"Daddy!" Jazi ran to the man standing at the bottom of the stairs. He swept her into his arms and kissed her curls.

A slim blonde, presumably Sierra, slipped past him and moved discreetly aside.

Lexi pushed to her feet along with everyone else. Dread swamped her at the displeasure stamped into his stone-hard features. Betrayal blazed in the gaze he leveled on her. This was why she wanted to be gone before he got here.

Clay stepped in front of her. "We invited them. We wanted to meet Jazi."

Eyes, sharp as black ice, cut to Clay. "And no one thought to call me? My daughter. My decision."

"You were in the air." Lexi slid forward, drawing his attention back to her. She wouldn't sacrifice his relationship with his brothers because of her decision. "And I wasn't staying for dinner, just for an hour. They had birthday presents for her."

"Oh, well then." Sarcasm dripped from the words. He set Jazi on her feet. "Can you go play with your presents? I need to talk to Lexi."

"'Kay." She ran over to Grace and the stack of packages.

"Jethro." Jackson strolled over and clapped Jethro on the shoulder. "Why don't you relax? Have a drink and some food. You just had a long flight after a couple of long days of meetings. We can work this out."

"There's nothing to work out. I just need to talk to Lexi."

Jethro grabbed her hand and led her up the stairs, through the foyer and out the front door.

"I can't believe you went behind my back to bring Jazi here. You knew I didn't want them involved in this business."

Business?

Anger came off him in waves, hotter than the desert sun shining down on them. She crossed her arms in front of her, but held her ground. "They weren't taking no for an answer."

"They didn't have to try too hard, did they? You've been angling to come here all week."

"That's not true." Her ire jacked up to match his, mixing with the hurt and betrayal she fought to contain. No way was she going to pay for his inability to communicate a simple response. "I've been asking what your plans were so I could make mine."

"You're not dense. You knew I didn't want you here."

"Which is why I gave up asking." She tried for calm. "I have a whole meal prepared for Jazi and me back at the hotel. Did I want to come spend the day with your friends? Yes. So when Clay came to get us, I may have put up less of a fight than I should have. But only because these people care about you and they think of your daughter as their niece."

Attempting to breach the gulf between them, she reached out a hand toward him. He jerked away from her touch.

"They want to know her so they can support you."

"There is no knowing her. Not when she's leaving." He slashed a hand toward the house. "These people are my family. I won't let you take them from me too. Won't let you destroy my life any more than you already have."

Every word shattered her heart more until nothing remained but pieces.

Devastated by his rejection, she retreated a step. Hope trickled away.

She closed her eyes, momentarily blocking out the world, but there was no blocking out the pain, no blocking out the sense of loss.

She opened her eyes, focused on the face she loved so dearly, and choked back a sob. He deserved so much more than he allowed himself. He just didn't know how to open himself to others so he drove them away. As he was driving her away.

"I feel so sorry for you. You're so worried about protecting your friends you don't see you're hurting them."

"You don't know what you're talking about."

"I know they love you. And it's their right to stand by you and help when you're suffering. When you refuse their support, you're telling them they don't matter."

"You're wrong. It's because they matter too much. I don't want them to suffer with me. And now they will. You brought Jazi here and now they'll love her. And they'll lose her too. That's on you."

"Oh, Jethro. You don't get to choose what people feel. They wanted to know her because she's a part of you. And even if she's not with you they can share your memories of her. Show them they matter. Introduce them to your daughter."

His features hardened to the point of granite. "I no longer have the option, do I? You've already done that."

"I haven't destroyed your life. You'll do that all on your own by pushing people away, the people who care about you. You say it's to protect them, but it's really to protect yourself. The problem with that is you'll be the one who loses out and the future is likely to be a very lonely place."

He cocked an arrogant brow. "I was fine until you came along."

How sad. He actually believed that.

"You want to know why I came here today? The truth?" Why not go out big? "I came because I hoped it didn't matter anymore. Fool that I am I fell in love with you. Making love with you was the most incredible thing I've ever done. I felt connected in a way I never have with anyone else. And I thought it was the same for you. That maybe we could be a family together, you, Jazi and foolish, foolish me."

Her throat closed up, cutting off her words. She shook her head, began backing away.

"You want to save them from being hurt? Quit pushing them away."

Heart rending, she turned her back on him and walked away.

Hard fingers wrapped around her elbow and swung her around. "Where are you going?"

"Anywhere but here. I'm leaving Jazi here. She loves you. If you care for her at all, you need to let her into your life or let us go."

"You're in no position to offer an ultimatum."

"You know me well enough to know I'll love her and care for her to the best of my ability. Unless you can come up with a new plan, the longer we stay, the harder it's going to be on her when we leave."

Yanking her arm from his grasp, she walked away.

Jethro stood in the driveway and watched Lexi storm away, knowing it was just for show. She'd said Clay came for her so she'd ridden here with him, and she didn't have her purse. No way she'd walk away without it.

Weary beyond belief, he rubbed the back of his neck. The break gave his tired mind time to catch up with the conversation. He needed a moment to breathe, to think. Lack of sleep dragged at him. A pounding headache reminded him he'd only gotten eight hours in three days.

Her statement about letting Jazi into his life confused and angered him. Something she excelled at. She had no business trying to change the terms of their agreement at this stage. From the beginning, she'd made it clear she wanted to take Jazi and leave. *He* wasn't invited to join the party. So why should she be surprised that he wanted to keep his family out of it?

She loved him? She wanted them to be a family?

He couldn't wrap his head around those possibilities.

Maybe he should have taken Jackson's advice to have a drink and settle down.

He'd been too hurt, too angry to listen. When he saw Lexi ensconced with his family, he saw red. He knew she longed for an invitation to Thanksgiving. He'd even considered it, because the thought of having all his family together appealed to him clear down to the bone.

But he knew he'd be a basket case when Lexi left with Jazi. From the beginning, he'd made it a priority to save his friends the same pain. Why was that a bad thing?

Lexi reached the last vehicle in the long drive. Stubborn woman, when was she going to give up this pretense? The sooner she returned, the sooner they could resolve this. Raw from walking in on a betrayal, he'd said some harsh things. Things he regretted. They'd talk more calmly when she came back.

Wait, he frowned, he didn't recognize the sporty little SUV. Panic set in when she stopped and pulled keys from her pocket.

"Lexi!" He started down the drive. Too late. She climbed

in, met his gaze for a brief second and then she threw the gear into Reverse, and was gone.

He trudged to a stop, hung his head. Something wrenched in his chest; the pain in her eyes ripped him in half. No telling how long he stood there before Jackson came out and fetched him. The others were gathered in the living room off the foyer. Grace wrapped him in a warm hug.

"Where's Jazi?"

"Sierra is with her in the game room. We want to talk to you." She led him to a cream sofa. "To say we're sorry. We pushed Lexi to bring Jazi here. She told Clay it wasn't a good idea, but we insisted. Jazi is your daughter—we wanted to know her."

Jethro perched on the edge of the sofa, stared down at the plush cream carpet. "Lexi said I was hurting all of you by not letting you see her. Was she right?"

Silence met his question. He looked up, met their gazes, shook his head. "Seems I'm the one who should apologize."

Grace laid a hand on his arm. "We don't understand why you won't let us help you."

"It's not about me. It's about you. All of you. I knew having Jazi stay with me was going to be tough. The truth is it's been brutal, harder than anything I've ever gone through. I wanted to spare you."

"Noble, but unnecessary," Ryan said. "Family stands together no matter how tough it gets."

A round of ascents echoed through the room.

"I should have known when you all tried to sneak by the penthouse and meet her that you weren't going to stay out of it."

"You knew about that?" Jackson grinned, clearly unrepentant.

"Lexi told me everything."

"I like her," Clay announced. "I didn't think I would, but I do."

"The problem is I do too. More than I should."

"Why is that a problem?" Grace demanded.

Back to scrutinizing the carpet. "She's leaving. Plus, you all know what a disaster I am at relationships."

Clay humphed. "You've never been in love before."

That brought his head up. "What are you talking about?"

"You love her." Ryan seconded Clay's declaration. "You look at her the way this poor sap looks at Grace. What's really telling is you've had the adoption contract for a month and can't bring yourself to sign it. Maybe I should be writing up a prenup instead."

Marriage to Lexi? Surprisingly the concept didn't throw him into a panic. Not like watching her drive away.

He'd missed her. He never missed people, taught himself at a young age not to bother. It didn't bring them back so it was wasted emotion. Worse, it was wasted energy. There'd only been one exception until now. Mama Harman. He still missed her.

And he'd missed Lexi. Missed her smile, the sweet smell of her hair, the exchange of glances when Jazi did something new. He missed how she teased him and the way she made him laugh. Most of all he missed the feel of her in his arms.

She'd spoken of a connection. He felt it too, the closeness, the chemistry, the bonding. With her he felt a sense of togetherness that chased the loneliness away. He just hadn't known what to call it.

"She said she loves me."

Jackson clapped him on the shoulder. "Then why are you still here?"

"Because I'm an idiot." He surged to his feet, pointed at Ryan. "You can forget the prenup."

"I'm not one to talk, but dude, don't deny yourself a chance at happiness."

"Oh. I'm going after her. And when I catch up with her, I'm never letting her go."

* * *

Lexi didn't remember the drive to the hotel. Between fighting off tears and struggling to breathe around the constriction in her chest she was lucky to make it back at all.

But she did make a decision. As painful as the confrontation had been, it revealed to her exactly what she needed to do.

She let herself into the suite and absorbed the quiet, the emptiness. Smelled the turkey and dashed away fresh tears. She set the key card down on the foyer table. She wouldn't be using it again.

Everything had changed. Just not as she'd hoped.

She loved Jethro.

Her breath hitched as she fought back unwanted tears. He didn't deserve them. She'd offered him her heart, told him of her dreams of becoming a family. Okay, she threw the words at him. But they'd been out there hanging in the balmy November day. And how did he respond? With harsh words and distrust.

In her room she went right through to the bathroom and splashed water on her face. The cool soothed the burn in her eyes. She began opening drawers and emptying them.

He'd accused her of destroying his life.

The woman in the mirror was the one shattered. Not only by his rejection, but because she knew in her heart of hearts that Jazi belonged with him.

Meeting her eyes in the mirror, she admitted she'd known it for a while. But today drilled the fact home. The look on his face when Jazi flew into his arms said it all. For that instant love broke through the anger and betrayal like the sun through rainclouds, lighting him up. Which made the ice he turned on her all the more devastating.

She dragged her suitcases out of the closet, opened them on the bed.

Her promise to Alliyah had become more of a crutch

than a motivator. Father and daughter loved each other, and much as Lexi would like to take Jazi and run, she couldn't justify it. The biggest thing she had to offer Jazi was love. And now she had that with her father.

Plus an aunt and a whole slew of uncles, all waiting to spoil her.

Uncaring of wrinkles, she began throwing things into the suitcases. Her heart couldn't be more broken; it only made sense to leave now. Make one big break. Let Jethro and Jazi begin their life together.

She swiped at her cheek, and stuffed her boots in the bigger case before zipping it. She had to lean her weight into it but she got it closed. Back in the bathroom she gathered her toiletries into a cosmetic bag. What didn't fit, she dumped in the other suitcase.

She wanted to be gone before Jethro got here. Which could be any minute considering how exhausted and angry he'd been. If he came home with Jazi before she left, Lexi feared she wouldn't have the strength to walk away.

And being in his life but not a part of it really didn't work for her. As painful as this was, it revealed to her exactly what she needed to do.

Silence met Jethro when he let himself in the suite.

He'd made a point of introducing Jazi to his friends. Lexi was right. They were his family and he wanted them to know his daughter. He wished Lexi had been there. As Jazi's mama, she was family too. Whether he got her to forgive him or not.

The place smelled of Thanksgiving. He stepped into the kitchen; it sparkled. But in the refrigerator a full turkey took up one shelf, and he saw carrots and potatoes. He hadn't answered her repeated queries about what they'd be doing, so she'd taken matters into her own hands. Had she planned for it to be just her and Jazi? Or had she hoped he'd join them?

He'd meant to. The stop at Jackson's was only to give a report and wish everyone happy Thanksgiving. And then he was going home. Because that's what Jazi and Lexi were to him. Home.

The pain and disappointment on Lexi's face continued to haunt him. Lord, help him, he needed to make this right.

But the silence told him she wasn't there. Just to be sure he checked her room. Dread burned through his belly, filled his heart. Her things were gone. Closet and drawers were empty. The bathroom cleared out. All that lingered was her scent, haunting him like a ghost.

Where would she have gone?

He headed out determined to find her. He'd try her apartment first. Then start tracking friends. Clay would help if needed.

That was when Jethro saw the note. On the foyer table right next to her key card.

Dearest Jethro,

I'm sorry for giving you an ultimatum today. That wasn't fair to either of us and I've come to cherish you as a friend.

You are a good man. I don't know what horrific circumstances forced your mother to give you up. But I can only think she'd be proud if she could see you today. Not for your financial success, though that's impressive, but because you are a man with a good heart.

Jazi belongs with you. She's happiest when you're around and she deserves to grow up with at least one of her parents. And you deserve to know the gift of your daughter's unconditional love.

You've restored balance to her world and she's brought joy to yours. I love the two of you too much to take one of you away from the other. So it's my place to bow out.

Forgive me for leaving this way. I don't think I could do it face-to-face.

Hugs and kisses to you both,

Lexi

P.S. Maybe you could bring her to see me dance some-day. I'd like that.

Raw emotion choked him. Lexi loved him. She'd told him so, but he hadn't believed her. Others had said the words and then left because he'd failed so miserably at commu-nication, at sharing himself. He shared with Lexi without even thinking about it. And she'd left, too, but by God, the sacrifice of it astounded him.

She thought his mother would be *proud* of him. Even after he tore her heart out and chased her away. Her crazy attempts to explain why he'd been in the trash had niggled at his psyche, causing some of the hostility to fade. He would never know the truth but it helped to contemplate a reason other than flat rejection by his mother.

Lexi thought she could tell him that and just walk away? That she could profess her love as if it didn't matter? Oh, no.

And suddenly he knew just where to find her.

Lexi's eyes stung from sweat and tears. Her image in the mirrors blurred from the moisture. But the music blasted, the beat rolled through her and she danced. She pushed all her sadness, her pain, her loneliness into each heart-felt motion.

She felt like she'd never be happy again, that she'd left her heart in the penthouse so far overhead.

She needed to get away, to make plans. Maybe she'd go to a new city, try out for a musical on Broadway. She was free, wasn't she, to do anything she wanted. That's what mattered. Right?

So why did her precious independence suddenly burn like acid in her belly? Why did having someone accept her for who she was suddenly seem like the true meaning of freedom?

Jethro had seen her, done things he didn't have to do. He found her a place to dance because he'd known she needed to dance. He'd introduced her to Veronica which gave her access to her world, and a chance at a new aspect of it. He'd arranged a jam session for her, negotiated for her to get credit for her participation.

Sway, pivot, lunge. Down, up, kick extend. Fast then slow and then faster still. Her feet pounded over the floor. Glided. Lifted her into the air. She danced until her legs shook and every breath became a labored effort.

Fatigue dragged her to a halt. Head down, chest heaving she finally let the tears come.

A moment passed, two when warm arms closed around her, holding her to a hard male body. Jethro's scent surrounded her.

"I'm sorry."

She went still. He'd come. He'd known where to find her. Everything in her longed to turn to him, to wrap around him. But he'd hurt her. She wasn't looking for pacification. She wanted love, a future.

"So sorry. I didn't mean the things I said. I was angry and tired from my trip. God's truth I don't remember half of it."

"Then why say it?"

He rested his chin on her head. "I don't know." His body went taut the full length of hers. "No, that's the old me. I want to do better with you." The words were flat as if squeezed through a tight throat. "When I came down the stairs and saw you there, I had this moment of absolute joy. Here was everything I'd ever longed for. And in the next instant it was wiped out because I'd promised to give it all up. And everyone I cared about was at risk."

"You lashed out."

"And you were the convenient target. I'm sorry. I don't remember much of what I said, but I do remember the hurt on your face." He rubbed his hands up and down her arms. Turned her to face him. With a gentle touch he wiped the tears from her face.

Heart pounding she stared up at him, half fearful, half hopeful. And, oh, my, she was so afraid to hope. What excited her was his effort, his openness. He was talking to her, a huge step for him. But would he make it all the way to a commitment?

"I take it back, all of it." Contrition stamped his features. "I talked to the guys after you left. You were right. They were feeling left out. They didn't need me to protect them. I took the time to officially introduce them to Jazi. Because family stands together."

"That's nice." She was happy for him. But it didn't change anything between them.

"I love you." Blunt. Declarative. Absolute. And so unexpected.

No way to doubt what she'd heard. To question his resolution. Happiness bloomed from her heart, warmed the chill from her blood, gave strength to her legs. She threw herself into his arms. He caught her, swung her around, sealed his lips to hers.

"I love you," she said against his mouth, "I love you. I love you."

He set her on her feet and stopped her talking in the best possible way. He pulled back, framed her face with hands that shook just a little.

"I want a family with you and Jazi. I want to give her a sister or brother, maybe both. I love you. Will you do that with me?"

She clasped his wrists, angled her chin up. "Are you going to require me to have an escort everywhere I go?"

His jaw clenched and his posture stiffened. Oh, he wanted to say yes. The fact he stopped to think showed his love as nothing else could.

"Were you serious about learning self-defense?"

Ah. Compromise, a relationship essential.

"I am if it gets rid of the babysitters."

"Then, no," he conceded. "Unless there's an imminent threat, you're free to roam at will."

Sweet, sweet words. She looped her arms around his neck. "Are we talking marriage? It's not a deal breaker for me, but it's probably best for the kids."

His eyes lit up. "You'd give your freedom up for me?"

See, he got her. "You and Jazi are my freedom. You don't contain me, you fulfill me."

"Then, Lexi Malone." He went down on one knee, held her hand in both of his. Looked up at her with such love. "Will you marry me?"

She cocked her head, pretended to consider? "Can we build a place by Jackson and Grace?"

He stood and yanked her into his arms. "This is not the time to tease me, woman."

"There's the man I know and love." She cupped his cheek, kissed him softly. "Yes, I'll marry you."

"Good." A huge grin broke across his face, revealing a dimple in his left cheek. "I already picked out the lot."

* * * * *

MILLS & BOON®
Hardback – September 2016

ROMANCE

To Blackmail a Di Sione	Rachael Thomas
A Ring for Vincenzo's Heir	Jennie Lucas
Demetriou Demands His Child	Kate Hewitt
Trapped by Vialli's Vows	Chantelle Shaw
The Sheikh's Baby Scandal	Carol Marinelli
Defying the Billionaire's Command	Michelle Conder
The Secret Beneath the Veil	Dani Collins
The Mistress That Tamed De Santis	Natalie Anderson
Stepping into the Prince's World	Marion Lennox
Unveiling the Bridesmaid	Jessica Gilmore
The CEO's Surprise Family	Teresa Carpenter
The Billionaire from Her Past	Leah Ashton
A Daddy for Her Daughter	Tina Beckett
Reunited with His Runaway Bride	Robin Gianna
Rescued by Dr Rafe	Annie Claydon
Saved by the Single Dad	Annie Claydon
Sizzling Nights with Dr Off-Limits	Janice Lynn
Seven Nights with Her Ex	Louisa Heaton
The Boss's Baby Arrangement	Catherine Mann
Billionaire Boss, M.D.	Olivia Gates

816 GEN STD HB

MILLS & BOON®
Large Print – September 2016

ROMANCE

Morelli's Mistress	Anne Mather
A Tycoon to Be Reckoned With	Julia James
Billionaire Without a Past	Carol Marinelli
The Shock Cassano Baby	Andie Brock
The Most Scandalous Ravensdale	Melanie Milburne
The Sheikh's Last Mistress	Rachael Thomas
Claiming the Royal Innocent	Jennifer Hayward
The Billionaire Who Saw Her Beauty	Rebecca Winters
In the Boss's Castle	Jessica Gilmore
One Week with the French Tycoon	Christy McKellen
Rafael's Contract Bride	Nina Milne

HISTORICAL

In Bed with the Duke	Annie Burrows
More Than a Lover	Ann Lethbridge
Playing the Duke's Mistress	Eliza Redgold
The Blacksmith's Wife	Elisabeth Hobbes
That Despicable Rogue	Virginia Heath

MEDICAL

The Socialite's Secret	Carol Marinelli
London's Most Eligible Doctor	Annie O'Neil
Saving Maddie's Baby	Marion Lennox
A Sheikh to Capture Her Heart	Meredith Webber
Breaking All Their Rules	Sue MacKay
One Life-Changing Night	Louisa Heaton

0816 GEN STD LP